The
Unravelling
of you

Books By J. A. Garth

Grief

Cassius

Guilt

Among The Umbra

Kingdom Of Secrets

Short stories

Becoming Maggie

Love Behind Her

The Anatomy of Us Series

The Unravelling of You

The Untangling of You

The Unravelling of you

J. A. Garth

Paperback ISBN: 978-1-7641330-0-5

Social Media:

FACEBOOK:

https://www.facebook.com j.ann.author

INSTAGRAM:

instagram.com j.a.garth_author

For my husband Nigel. I never could have written a single word, let alone multiple books, without you. Thank you for being such an incredible husband, father and my biggest fan.

Prologue

I'm not a praying man. But looking down at her in this state, her soft ivory skin completely naked, her chestnut hair cascading over her skin like silk and her lips so expertly wrapped around my cock I can't help but think I should thank whatever deity it was who sent her practically falling onto me on that plane. This beautiful, impossible, courageous woman who I have just allowed into my fucked-up mess of a world against all better judgment, has turned my world on its head.

She grazes her teeth along my length, and I lose all sense. If I were a better man, I would have ignored her fluttering eyelashes, her cheeks going red every time she lingered just a little too long at me and her soul seeing green eyes that completely disarm me. God, I long to turn other parts of her skin red under my hand.

My poor lawyer is going to lose his shit when he finds out I haven't requested an NDA from her. I'm not usually this stupid. I know the importance of them. Hell, I'm dealing with the consequences as we speak, even after making Autumn sign one. No, I bought her in here to help her forget about that shit. I need this just as much as I need it for her. Her tongue flicks over the slit at the end of my knob.

"Fuck, Sam." I damn near finish on the spot. All thoughts of Autumn, her fist connecting with my nose, her hands around my throat, the smashed-up glass table and dinnerware across my kitchen and living room and the smell and feel of my blood pouring from my nose are a distant, blurred memory. Right now, there is only me and the little siren between my legs with the entirety of my cock down her throat.

One

I groan at the practically empty fridge and wonder how creative I can get with butter, raspberry jam, a block of cheese that is probably still good, and a head of lettuce that definitely isn't. There's no way around it; I'm going to have to stop in and do some groceries after work this morning if I plan on eating tonight. I close the fridge, admitting defeat. No breakfast this morning, it is, again. My white sheer curtains dance playfully with the breeze that flows through the open kitchen window. It fills the kitchen with the smell of pine from the trees that line the sides and back of the property.

The old farmhouse walls creak tiredly, and a group of birds gather in a tree not too far out from my kitchen window and bring in the morning sun with a song I'm sure some people would find beautiful, but to me, right now, it's the most irritating sound I've ever heard.

The early morning chill nips at my skin and, with a grumble, I pull my robe tighter around me. I contemplate lighting the fire and enjoying my morning tea in front of it, but I know I would be wasting my time. I need to get upstairs now if I want time to shower, do my makeup and eat before work. Trust me to land a job on one side of town while living in a house that is twenty minutes out from the other side. Factor in traffic, and I spend an average of two hours in the car every day going to and from. With another annoyed grumble, I reluctantly slide my robe off. I take a glance at the clock over the mantle, that is going to tell me what I already know. It's six thirty AM. My body clock started falling into the routine of my work schedule pretty quickly after I started my job at INSPIRE TELCOM call centre two years ago.

I make my way upstairs, almost every step creaks and protests under the weight of my feet. Just one of the many charms of my hundred-year-old hideaway farmhouse. The other is the fact that no matter how hard I try, I can never have more than one room warmed up from the fireplace in the living room. On the coldest nights through winter, I sleep on the sofa by the fire to keep warm. It's old, it has its flaws, but it's my home, and I love it. Especially when the weather is warm enough to have all the windows open instead of just one out of necessity to ensure airflow through the house. The summer breeze and light seem to bring life back into my home.

Just as I take the last step at the top of the staircase, there is a knock at the door. I jump, startled by the unexpected sound and hold my hand to my chest.

What the hell?

"Sam, come open the door already, my hands are full."

My body sags with relief at the sound of Alisha, my best friend's voice. I'm also a little impressed that she has managed to make her voice carry so clearly all the way upstairs. I go back downstairs to unlock the door and let her in.

"What on earth are you doing here this early? I didn't even know you knew this time of morning existed." I say with a chuckle. I roll my eyes at the sight of her. She's perfectly in place. Blonde hair styled in a blowout, blue jeans that hug her just right, a cute white milkmaid style top and an unbuttoned dusty pink cardigan that's doing its very best, I'm sure to keep her warm.

"So, you don't want freshly baked muffins from that little store near your work?"

My eyes are drawn first to the bag she is holding up and waving around, then to the other two she has in her other hand.

"Depends," I say, shifting my weight and putting my left hand on my hip. "Are they still warm?"

"Not for much longer if you keep making me stand out here in this damn cold." She playfully chastises.

"Alright, come in then."
I move out of the doorway and let her pass before closing the door behind her. Then, I follow her into the kitchen.

"What's with the rest of the bags?"

"English breakfast or Earl Grey? She asks, getting herself an English breakfast.

"Same as you," I say dismissively and lean over the butcher block counter to grab one of the bags.

"Wait!" she shouts suddenly and snatches the bags away.

"I want a muffin," I say, pouting. The scent of cinnamon, chocolate and apple is starting to penetrate through the bag, making my stomach rumble and my mouth water.

"I need you to promise you won't be mad." If there is anything to know about my best friend, it's that any time she says not to be mad, she's outdone herself with something that is guaranteed to piss you off.

"What did you do, Alisha Quinn?" I say, raising an eyebrow.

"Listen. Not. Hear." She says, this time facing me.

Her face is full of worry, and she's fidgeting with the tips of her fingers. Neither of us has pulled the listen, not hear card in months. The last time it was used was when she was thinking about moving hours away with her boyfriend, she had been with for around a year and who I had never even seen a photo of. Thank God he had apparently managed to convince her to stay here. Something about the whole thing didn't sit right with me, and I would absolutely hate for something bad to happen to her, not to mention her mother would probably hunt me down with a pitchfork if I let her daughter run off with someone none of us have met.

"We've spoken about this, Alisha. It's a rule we made as teenagers; we don't need to evoke it now as adults. I would like to think we are a little more mature now."

"Listen, not, hear." She repeats. This time her words are sharp.

"Alright, geez, just tell me what's in the damned bags already.

She makes quick work of making the cups of tea now that the kettle has finished boiling. She sets mine down on the counter in front of me and curls her fingers around her mug, then stares at the tea bag as if lost in thought. Her blue eyes dart a little, and tiny frown lines form around her lips.

"Alisha, I have to start getting ready for work. Please, just tell me what's going on."

She takes a deep-centring breath and takes a sip of her tea.

"I came over the other day while you were at work."

"Okay?" I say, curious but not concerned, I gave her a key to my place, assuming there would be times that she would be here when I wasn't.

"I needed to borrow those cute ankle boots you bought a few weeks back, but have been too busy to try out for yourself. I had a lunch date with mum, and they were perfect for a new dress I wanted to wear."

"You ruined them and bought me a replacement pair?" I ask, guessing the most likely thing that has happened. No wonder she seems so nervous to tell me, I would be too; those were expensive.

"No, the boots are fine, they're at home, I will bring them back, I just need to borrow them one more time before I do." She says quickly. "On my way out, I wanted to grab a bottle of water from the fridge, when I did that, I noticed you had almost nothing in there, nothing besides absolute basics anyway. You can't live off bread, butter, eggs, milk and whatever leftovers you have from take-out. So" she pauses for a moment and looks like she is studying me for my reaction. I do my best to keep my cool so she can continue, and after a slow exhale, she does. "I got you some groceries. Nothing too much, just enough to do you for the next few days until I have some free time to come shopping with you. Maybe you will be more inclined to *actually* do it if you're not alone."

Her admission takes me by surprise. The contents of my fridge really aren't something she needs to worry about. Admittedly, I haven't done a full shop for a while, but I haven't needed anything. I can feel myself frowning, and it pisses me off.

"That really wasn't necessary."

"It was, Sam. I'm worried about you; you never go out anymore, you're either at home or at work. That's what every single day for the last two months has looked like for you. You need to get out of here; you need to meet people and buy some damn groceries."

Her words are loud and blunt, but her expression is soft. I want to be mad; I want to cuss her out for deciding that my life isn't good enough because it doesn't look like hers. I want to tell her to take her groceries and shove them. But I can't. It's not worth the energy of an argument.

"Thank you for the groceries. I promise you, I'm fine. I will stop in to get some more stuff on the way home tonight." I say, with what I hope is a reassuring smile.

She starts loading up my fridge with the contents of the bags, some fresh fruit and vegetables, some chicken that she puts in the freezer, cheese, yoghurt and a couple of other things I don't see. Once she has finished, she pulls the muffins out and sets them up on a plate for each of us.

"Thank you." I say, peeling back the paper and taking a bite of the now barely warm apple cinnamon muffin. It is absolutely divine, even still, after it has cooled.

There's a new guy. The thought takes my attention from my muffin for just a second.

"So, tell me." I say between bites, "Do I get to meet this one?"

"Who?" she asks, but something about the way she looks at me makes me think she knows exactly what I'm talking about.

"The cute guy you stole my boots for. Do I get to meet him?"

"I told you; I used them for lunch with my mum." She shrugs dismissively.

"Ah, huh." I smile and shake my head. I've known her long enough to know that the only reason she would drive all the way across town to find a pair of my boots is for a guy.

Her dating history already tells me the answer to my question, though. There is zero chance of me meeting this guy. I take a sip of my tea and shake my head again.

"Forgive me for not believing you, but you were with the last guy for nearly a year, and I never got to meet him. That's not something best friends usually do to each other. You're holding out on me Alisha Quinn, and sooner or later, I'm going to figure out why." I say with a chuckle and wash down my now finished muffin with more of my tea.

"He wanted to keep us private; I've told you that a million times now. I just wanted to respect his wishes."

"Do you really still have to respect his wishes if you're not together anymore? You won't even tell me why you broke up."

"I will, it's just still too soon."

I agree to waiting until she is ready and put my dirty dishes in the sink, giving them a quick rinse.

"I have to go get ready for work now, or I'm going to be late. Stay and finish your tea if you want. And thank you for the groceries."

I give her a small smile and rush up the stairs. I round up my clothes for the day and glance at the clock on the bedside table.

Damn.

I guess washing my hair will have to wait until tonight.

I'm showered, dressed, and hair and makeup done within thirty minutes. I double-check that I have locked the house when I notice that Alisha has left and get in the car, throwing my handbag and a bottle of water onto the passenger seat.

Just get through today.

I repeat the words over and over, finally working up the courage to pull out onto the highway.

Two

I pull into the parking lot with ten minutes to spare. By some miracle, I find a park reasonably close to the five-story concrete building with the words IN-SPIRE TELCOM above the double door entry. I grab everything I need from the passenger seat, rush inside and head straight for the elevator. Barely managing to make it to one that was just about to close, with only one other person inside. I think I have seen him around before; he works in the IT department on the third floor.

"Which floor?" he asks quietly.

"Fifth, please."

He presses the button for the fifth floor, and the doors close.

"System's a little slow this morning. So unfortunately, you lot are going to be a little backed up on customers, I'd imagine." He says apologetically.

That's just great.

"Thanks for letting me know," I say, trying to keep my annoyance to myself. Obviously, it's not this guy's fault that something is wrong. But I'm sure as hell Yates is going to make it mine.

"All good." He says, then answers his ringing phone. The doors open to the third floor, and he steps out. The doors close behind him, and a few moments later, they open up to my floor. I make quick work of getting set up at my desk and logging in to my computer, ready to start taking calls, *hopefully*.

"How's his mood today?" I ask Nicki as she hangs up from the call she was on when I sat down. Her blush pink lips pull into a straight line, and her perfectly manicured eyebrows crease at the bridge of her nose.

"You mean Mr. jerk-off? How do you think he is? The same way he's been all week." She shakes her head.

"It's only Tuesday, how are we supposed to get through the rest of the week if he keeps this up. He is such a tyrant pig." I say, more to myself than Nicki. But she still hears me just fine.

"I know, and yet it feels like I've been under his wrath for at least the last three consecutive days. It's worse today because everything is running really slow."

"Yeah, I heard. That bad, huh?" I frown.

"Yeah, that bad. Get logged in and start picking up some of this slack. The calls are coming through okay. But you're going to have to pen and paper as much of the info as you can until we can get back into the customer accounts portal properly. That seems to be where the main problem is. On our end and theirs." She is already turning back to her screen.

"Yeah, I'm on it." I say and pull out a pen and a notepad.

***

By midday, the system is finally running smoother, and we have managed to get a handle on the number of calls getting backed up.

I take a minute before answering the next call on the line to have a drink of water and notice that I have a message from Alisha. I am about to pick it up and read it, but before I do, instinctively, I look up to make sure the coast is clear. *Crap, he's coming this way.*

I discreetly tap Nicki on the arm.

"He's coming. Be ready." I whisper, and both of us busy ourselves with our work. I pick up the waiting call and immediately jump into action. Making sure he can see I am busy, and whatever he is coming over to say will have to wait.

"Good morning, you've reached INSPIRE, my name is Samantha, what can I help you with to-day?"

The woman on the other end of the line explains that she is having some trouble with her internet connection and needs it fixed as soon as possible because she is expecting a video call from her grandchildren in the next few hours, who live in another town.

"I am very sorry to hear about that, Mrs Jones. Let's try to get you back up and running so you don't miss out on seeing those grandbabies of yours. Before we begin, can I please confirm your identity and account details?"

Mr Yates positions himself behind me, close enough that the stench of cigarettes and stale beer fills the air around me. My nose twitches, and I focus on Mrs Jones, who is reading out her account number and confirming all the questions I am asking her.

He leans in closer, close enough that his warm breath is on the back of my ear. He puts his weight down on the back of my seat, and I resist the urge to shove it out from under his hands.

I input the information Mrs Jones is providing and gain access to her account. There is a box attached to her account that is letting me know she has missed her last payment, so her internet has been shut off until the payment is made.

Mr Yates removes one of his hands from the back of my seat and places it on my shoulder, giving it a light squeeze.

I talk my way through the anger, somehow keeping my tone level. I inform Mrs Jones of the payment that is in arrears, and I begin the process with her to make the payment over the phone right away. She apologises for forgetting and promises it won't happen again. I help her make the payment and repeat everything we have done today while she has been on the phone, needing her to confirm that I have done everything it is she has wanted me to do today.

The call is coming to an end, which means I am going to have to talk to Mr Yates. I thank Mrs Jones for her patience and end the call.

Here we go.

"Good morning, Mr Yates, is there something I can help you with?" I say as politely as I can through a gritted smile.

"No, I'm just checking in, seeing how you *lovely* ladies are getting on for today. Especially after such a hectic morning." A slick smile spreads across his face, and his eyes darken as his gaze flicks from my face down to my breasts and back again. Wordlessly, he licks his lips, and my stomach churns. *Bring back the tyrant, I prefer him over the pig.* He raises his eyebrow and crosses his arms over his chest. I'm taking too long to answer.

"We are doing just fine, thank you." Another call comes through on my line.

Thank God.

"I should get this, so if there isn't anything else?" I say, with my hand already hovering over the answer button.

"No, that's all, keep up the good work." He says and gives Nicki a look thick with desire before stalking back toward his office.

"Fucking creep." Nicki says, disgusted.

I nod in agreement and answer the call.

As soon as I hang up, I remember the message from Alisha.

Alisha: How goes the

life of an internet

provider, call centre

worker?

I roll my eyes and send a quick reply.

Me: Stimulating as

ever, for some of

us more than others —

She doesn't reply right away, so I move on to the

next call.

Three

Reluctantly, I get my bag out of the car and head into the grocery store. It was sweet of Alisha to be concerned this morning, but buying me groceries was unnecessary. I'm not sure what she thinks is wrong with me, but whatever her assumption is, it's wrong. I can afford my groceries, and I do eat. I just can't stand being stuck in the damn grocery store for more than a few minutes, and doing a full shop would mean doing that.

I weave through the other customers in the store, getting only what I know I am going to need for at least a week. Hopefully, that will be enough to get Alisha off my back. Twenty minutes later, I am out of the store, have loaded my groceries into the back of my car and head home to the quiet.

The afternoon traffic is a nightmare — I turn the radio on to try and help the drive seem not so bad, but it's a useless attempt at distraction.

You need to report Yates. The voice in my head stubbornly demands, again.

I have lost count of the number of times I have had this battle with myself. Of course, I know I need to report him, I'm certainly not the only one, and I am sure there are women who experience his inappropriate and creepy behaviour far worse than me. But every single woman who has stood up against him so far was packing their desk by that same afternoon. They were told it wasn't because they had reported him, of course. It was usually something along the lines of their performance review was in the red, or they need to let go of staff due to budget cuts. Until I can guarantee I have another job lined up, I'm stuck. Just like the rest of the women on his payroll.

After an hour and fifteen minutes, I finally get home, I lug the groceries inside, turn on the Bluetooth speaker and fill the room with music as I pack everything away.

The music cuts off suddenly, and I realise it's because Alisha is calling me.

"Hey." I say, putting the now empty grocery bags away.

"Did you get groceries?"

"Yes, ma'am." I say sarcastically.

"I'm glad to hear it. Listen, I have something exciting to tell you."

"Okay?" I ask. Suspicious. Alisha and I have *vastly* different views on what the word exciting means.

"I booked both of us in for a holiday on the Gold Coast, you, me, beaches, a gorgeous hotel and just the right number of bars to have the best chance of meeting *Prince Charming*."

To my surprise, it sounds wonderful, travelling to the other side of the country and escaping it all for a minute, getting to just run away, is exactly what I need right now, but only in theory. It's unrealistic. I can't just decide on a whim to go on a holiday.

"I don't know... I mean, I can't just pack up and leave, I have to work, besides, didn't you just start dating someone? Why do you need to meet some-one else?" I smile as I hope the trap I set works. I know damn well she is seeing someone.

"He was a lost cause." She says quickly. I roll my eyes at her admission.

"You have to come, Sam. I already booked and paid for everything."

I sigh, frustrated. I really don't understand how she can expect me to put my life on hold at the drop of a hat, like I don't have commitments.

"I will try to put in for the time off, but I doubt Yates is going to approve it."

"He's the whole reason I'm making you take this damn holiday. It's not right, Sammie. You can't stay there. I hear we have some openings coming up at work. Let me put your name in."

"I will think about it, just tell me how long I need to put in for my leave."

The line goes silent.

"Alisha?"

"We leave this Friday." She paused again. "For two weeks."

The air is sucked from my lungs. I love this girl to pieces, but I swear it's her life's mission to see what it would take to cause me a heart attack.

"What? Alisha, what the hell are you thinking? I can't leave for that long, he would never approve it and forgetting that for a second, how in the hell did you get that kind of money?"

I know the answer as soon as I ask the question.

"Alisha, you didn't..."

"I can replace it. It's fine." She says quickly.

"Alisha, you have been saving that money for a house for nearly two years. You've done so well. Why would you ruin it now?"

"It wasn't that much." She says, but it sounds like she is trying to convince herself more than me.

"How much isn't that much?"

"I needed to pay for return flights, fourteen nights at the hotel, plus money for food and other necessities, then of course money so we can have a little fun…"

"How much Alisha?"

"Twenty thousand." She says, just a little louder than a whisper.

"Alisha Quinn, last I heard you had sixty saved. Why on earth would you use so much?" I chastise, horrified.

"It's fine, like I said, I can replace it. Plus, most of it is just emergency money. And accommodation for such a long stay was nearly half of that. I will just try to pick up some extra shifts when we get back so I can replace it sooner rather than later. Voluntarily picking up shifts should translate well for that manager position that came up."

My god, she can be exasperating, but then, it's not fair of me to be surprised. She's always been like this, since the five years I've known her, anyway.

"Well, you're not going to replace it by yourself. Let me pay back half of it for you. It's only fair." I know I'm wasting my time with the offer, but it doesn't feel right to have her spend all of this money on the both of us.

"Samantha, really, you know that's not necessary. Besides, this holiday is more for me. It just wouldn't be much of one if I didn't have my best friend with me."

"Alisha Quinn, you are Impossible."

"Love you too, anyway, I have to go, I'm going out again tonight. You're welcome to join me?"

"You know it's not my thing." I say politely.

"I know, I know. Just thought I'd ask. Enjoy falling in love with whatever dreamboat is in whatever book you're reading at the moment. I'm going to try my luck meeting real men with real bodies I can really lather up with baby oil and…"

"Okay, I'm hanging up now. Be safe and make good choices."

"Bye, boring." She says with a chuckle that makes me shake my head.

"Bye Alisha."

I hang up my phone and let out an exhausted yawn. Every conversation with her usually leaves me feeling sluggish.

I shake my head again, both at her behaviour and the fact that she knows me too well. I had planned on bringing in the night with a book by the fire, paired with a light dinner. But now, just to show her, I want to do something else, not go out of course, but something. I rub my finger on my chin in contemplation, but really, I know there is nothing else I want to be doing. She can have her real men. Mine don't come with baggage, mistrust, and they are rarely capable of hurting me. Wait, there is something I can do. Alisha was right, I need this, I need a break, I need to get away from work for a while and away from Mr Yates, I need a fresh mind, one that I can hopefully use well enough when I come back to get a job somewhere else. I can't remember the last time I packed up and left, besides going to visit my mother, but that's only an hour away. I'm taking the time off, even if that means quitting and finding a new job as soon as I can when I return. I have some money built up in my emergency fund. I can use that responsibly to get by until I get a new job.

Easy there, he might approve your leave.

I scoff at the thought. *Yeah, right.*

It's settled, I won't be reading tonight, I will be packing. My excitement takes me by surprise. I bound up the stairs two at a time with a stupidly massive grin. Maybe it is time to meet a real man. One that I can meet on the beach, or at a bar, one that I can put back where I found him when it's time for me to come home and not let myself worry about all the complications that come with an actual partner. The thought is devilish and very unlike me

— it's a thought that makes me feel giddy, confused, and hungry. All in one.

I rummage through my drawers looking for things to pack, and my wide smile slowly turns to a frown. I need to go shopping. Nothing I have in my wardrobe is going to suit my master plan. Alisha is going to be thrilled. I rush back downstairs and pick up my phone.

Me: Cancel your plans for
 the night, we're going
 shopping.

She replies faster than I expected.

Alisha: Samantha, I love you.
 But I am not cancelling my
 plans to pick up groceries with
 you. (Although I am VERY
 happy to hear that you're going to
 get some.)

What? She already knows I did my groceries. I roll my eyes at myself. I know better than to think she didn't already forget all about the non-exciting part of our conversation. I opt for calling her, knowing that she's already likely bored with my messages and is unlikely to read the next message I send until she is finished getting herself ready.

After six rings, she finally picks up.

"I think you can handle doing this alone, sweetie. If you need me to come with you, we will go tomorrow. I know you have enough food to get you by for longer than that."

I roll my eyes at her through the phone.

"I don't want to do groceries, Alisha. I already did that on my way home today. I told you that already. It was awful, thanks for wondering."
She lets out an impatient groan.

"What do you need to shop for then?'"

"Holiday outfits, new bikini, that sort of thing."

"Wait, did I hear that right? Samantha Locket is swapping out a one-piece and oversized shirt for a bikini?"

Now I've got her interest.

"Yeah, it's not that big of a deal." I say quietly, already starting to regret my sudden burst of confidence. "Only if you think I should?" I ask nervously.

"Are you kidding me? It's about time you showed the world just how ridiculously hot that body of yours is. I never understood why you insisted on hiding yourself so much. I'm coming to get you; I've already got my keys in my hand. I know just where we need to go." She's shouting, and I have to move the phone away from my ear to avoid a burst eardrum.

"I will see you when you get here, just don't make such a huge deal out of it." I ask, gently pleading.

"But this is a big deal!"

"Alisha, please."

"Fine, I will see you soon. Make sure you're ready to go."

"See you soon." I say and hang up. I consider changing, but don't bother. The black jeans and powder blue button-up I wore to work today will work fine. I just need a jacket now that the cool air is settling in. I go find one and slip it on, then grab my purse and double-check to make sure I have my ID on me. Maybe we could go for dinner and wine when we are finished shopping, at least Alisha will still get to have a drink like she had planned. Honestly, though, I don't know how she does it. It's a Tuesday night, and she has work tomorrow. No wonder she complains she can never find anyone decent enough for her when she's out. What does she expect when most people are usually at home and saving their weekends for that sort of thing?

For what feels like the twentieth time today, I silently shake my head at her.

My phone rings, surprising me. That can't be her already letting me know she's here, it's a half-hour drive at least, during good traffic.

I locate my phone and answer it. It's her.

"Everything okay?"

"No, it's not, I'm sorry, but I can't hang out tonight. Something has come up. Can we reschedule for tomorrow? I can pick you up from work?"

I feel utterly deflated, more than I had expected. I was looking forward to spending the night shopping with her and trying something bold and new.

"Yeah, it's fine." I say, trying to hide my disappointment. "Is everything okay?"

"Yeah, I can't talk about it right now. But I will give you a call tomorrow. Make sure you tell the creep you're leaving for your holiday. If you won't, I will when I come pick you up."

I would laugh, but I know she isn't joking. She would not hesitate to make the arrangements happen, not backing down until he approved of them. Maybe I should just get her to ask in the first place?

Samantha, you are a grown — arse woman. Act like it.

"Don't worry, I will get it sorted, you just make sure you call me in the morning so I know you're okay and so you can tell me what's going on."

"Course I will, night babe."

"Goodnight Alisha."

Well damn.

I guess Alisha was right, after all, a book by the fire it is. Maybe this is for the best. I will come to my senses by morning and realise I really shouldn't waste my time shopping for things I won't end up wearing. I know when it comes time to, I will end up opting for what is comfortable and familiar. A one-piece and oversized tee. I'm not cut out for laying on a beach somewhere in a bikini, the sun kissing my skin, making it bronze and beautiful. I wasn't blessed with the type of skin that likes to cooperate in those situations. Mostly it just goes beet red, and I spend the next few weeks tending to the completely un worth it, painful blisters and peeling skin.

I pout a little as I gather some kindling from the bucket by the fire and the box of matches. With more ease than usual, I get the fire started and gradually add bigger pieces of wood until I am satisfied. I hold my hands out close to the growing flames that flicker beautifully, its orange glow spilling out into the living room behind me. The room fills with the smell of smoke and burning wood, and I inhale deeply. The warmth in my hands is gradual and comforting; it stretches its way up my arms, and my body shivers, getting used to the sudden mix of temperatures. As soon as I am satisfied that I have warmed myself up enough, I kick off my shoes and pull off my jacket and jeans.

I sigh, frustrated at the realisation that I'm still going to have to go upstairs to change my shirt. Begrudgingly, I change into a cotton camisole but sigh in relief when I remove my bra. I grab my duvet and the book from the top of my nightstand and make my way back downstairs. I take care to watch my footing; I have taken a tumble down these stairs many more times than I'd like to admit. Especially when I've been carrying things like my duvet down. I collect my phone from the kitchen counter on my way past, noticing an unread message as I do.

I take a seat on my sofa, it's seen better days, not since I've had it. I got it second-hand at a yard sale not long after I moved in. I'm sure it was beautiful when it was originally purchased. It's once vibrant red, now a dull, almost brown. I have made attempts to clean it, but so far, it's been to no avail. Maybe I should admit defeat, just like both Alisha and my mother have told me to and buy a new one. Perhaps when I get back from the holiday.

Sure, if you still have a job to come back to, so you can afford a new one.

I check the unanswered message, assuming it would be from Alisha, but it's from my mother.

Mum: Evening, dear, just checking
in. Your Dad and I are well.
I do hope you're looking after
yourself, and you aren't
committing yourself too much
to that dreadful boss
of yours.

I never planned to let my mother know about Mr Yates and his behaviour. But she had come to surprise me at home one afternoon with a visit, when she walked in, I had been crying. The stress of the day, in general, was topped off by his advances being particularly incessant that day. I hadn't expected to, but on my drive home, the closer I got to home I broke. When I walked in my front door, and she saw me all teary and puffy-eyed, I had to tell her. I did consider lying, but she would have known. She always knows.

Me: Hey, Mum, I'm doing fine.
Thanks for checking in.
Work is the same as it always
Is, but I am hoping it won't be
a problem for much longer.
Alisha and I are leaving for a
while to get away from it all.
I will call you tomorrow.
Love you. x

I look down at the book that is sitting on the floor by the sofa. I go to pick it up, but stop myself. I can already tell my mind isn't in it, and I will just be stuck rereading the same line over and over until I inevitably give up.

I slump back onto the sofa and stare at the ceiling. The years have not treated it well. The white is a mix of yellows and greys, blending together in parts. My eyelids grow heavy, and I welcome the darkness as it wraps itself around me.

***

I wake violently shivering. My upper back is aching, and I can see every breath I am taking.

Damn it.

The fire is out, and I have kicked the blanket off. I pick it up and wrap it around myself as tightly as I can and snuggle into it. The blanket is cold, and I groan, frustrated. After a few minutes, I am finally warm again. I close my eyes, grateful at the very moment my phone begins to ring.

Who in the world?

It's a stupid question, I know there is only one person who would be calling me at this hour, *whatever hour it currently is*. I consider letting it go to voicemail, but the last time I spoke to her, she was dealing with what seemed to be some kind of emergency. I need to answer. My reluctance because I want to stay warm isn't going to win this time, not when I know something could be wrong.

The icy air stings my exposed arm, that I use to pick up my phone from the floor.

Before I answer, I take note of the time.

Damn it, again. I have to get up for work.

I sit up and answer the phone.

"Are you okay?" I ask, my voice broken from both the cold and the sleep that I'm not finished with.

"Sammy!" she whines. "I have the worst news."

I slump back down at the sound of her whine and throw my arm over my face and cover my eyes.

"What's happened?" I ask, accidentally sounding disinterested.

"I can't go on our holiday!"

"Oh?" and just like that, I am sitting up again, this time far more disappointed than I thought I would be hearing those words.

"That's okay, we can try another time."

"No, you didn't hear me right. I said *I* can't go. *You* are still taking this holiday."

"Alisha, I'm not going on your holiday without you."

"You have to, you don't have a choice. The hotel reservation was non-refundable. Besides, I'm still going to try to make it. I can't come because of a work thing. I will try to pull some strings and will hopefully be there still, just a few days late."

It takes me a minute to be able to answer her, I mean, could I take a holiday by myself? Hours away from anyone I know? Even if it is only for a few days, it's still way out of my comfort zone.

"Samantha, stop it. I can hear you overthinking this. You need to do this for you. This holiday was for the both of us. We both need a break. I know I said it was for me, but we both know you need this so much more than I do."

"I don't know Alisha ... Are you sure you can't leave on Friday?"

"Yeah, I'm sure. Look, I know this isn't ideal for either of us. But look at it this way, if you do this, you are actually doing me a huge favour. If I try to cancel and re-book, I will lose so much money. This way, I don't have to worry about that. So please, do this for me."

"I... okay, fine."

I'm going to regret this.

"You're the best. I promise to get to you as soon as I can. But I need you to promise me that you will allow yourself to have a good time and actually try to relax. You know, do the thing that is the whole purpose of me wanting to steal you away."

Pinch the bridge of my nose to ease the building tension.

"I promise to do my absolute best to be someone I'm not for the sake of making you feel like I have relaxed and enjoyed myself to your satisfaction," I say, snickering.

"You are such a smart arse." She says, joining me in my laughter.

"Alright, I have to go. I will let you know I anything changes."

"Make good choices." I say and hang up the phone.

Getting ready for work and forcing myself to build up any sort of motivation to deal with the shit show that is guaranteed to greet me at the elevator has been a challenge from the very first day Mr Yates decided to try to stick his claws in. But today is worse, today I don't need to just put on a smile and be polite. I need to ask him for something, and the knotting in my stomach confirms what I already know, he is going to ask for something in return, and if I decline, today could very well be the last day I walk through those doors. This is what today is going to come to, allow myself to get fired for rejecting my boss's advances or quit, not allowing them to happen in the first place.

I glare, frustrated at the line-up of cars in front of me, moving at a snail's pace. I get a chill and re-alise it's darker outside than it should be. A thick grey cloud blankets the town, threatening to dump rain over us at any second.

How hadn't I noticed until now?

I glare at the sky and turn on both the heater and radio. The car warms up in no time, but unfortu-nately, my mood never does. I try to pay attention to the news lady on the radio, but I can hardly hear her over the sound of my own thoughts playing out different scenarios for how this morning is going to go. I consider, for a moment, calling in sick for the day and asking for the time off at the same time.

Coward.

I grip the steering wheel tighter and finally reach my turn-off. I weave through the streets and pull into work, this time with fifteen whole minutes to spare. I turn the engine off once I have found a vacant park and sit back in my seat, resting my head against the headrest and sigh. I close my eyes tight and try to find enough courage to walk through those doors, ask for what I am entitled to and accept the consequences. Whatever they may be.

The elevator is empty when the doors open and I am the only one waiting out the front of this particular one. I appreciate the last few moments I get to have alone to pull myself *and my thoughts* together before I reach my floor.

Far too quickly, the doors open up again, and I am out of time.

I rush to my desk next to Nicki, who is only just logging in for the day.

"Morning." She says with a warm smile, but doesn't look away from her screen.

"Is he in his office?" I ask, desperately hoping she says no. If he's busy elsewhere, I can continue to source the courage I am still yet to find.

"The beast? Yeah, for now. He should be out in the next fifteen for the morning briefing."

"Damn it."

"Why?" She asks, now looking at me. I want to grumble at how put-together she looks for so early in the morning. I envy her ability to have her blonde hair perfectly pinned back into a high pony. Not a single strand appears out of place, and makeup so well done. If she's got any imperfections going on I wouldn't know it.

"I'm going to ask to use the time off I've accumulated."

"You can't," she says. Her pleading tone taking me by surprise. We had grown close enough working beside each other after all this time, but I hadn't considered the very likely event of being fired or quitting would affect her.

"I have to, everything is already booked."

"You booked without knowing if he would approve you?" She shakes her head, and her ponytail sways slightly.

"Well, no. I didn't — Alisha did."

"Hmm." She responds, not bothering to hide her disapproval.

I ignore her repugnance of my best friend, as I often do. I get that Alisha can seem a little *much* to people who don't know her well enough, but after years of friendship, she has developed into being my person. Even if most others who meet her don't manage to see beyond the shield she puts up around herself.

I sit at my desk, log in and open my emails. I scan through the handful of emails that have come through since I left last night.

"Good morning, everyone." Simon Yates says, managing to make his voice reach across the entirety of the room.

The room falls silent, and everyone's eyes are directed at him.

"I have been asked to remind everyone to label their food in the refrigerator and to ensure you are cleaning up after yourself. That includes doing the dishes." His eyes narrow as he takes the time to look around the room before continuing.

"The systems are back up and running at full capacity after yesterday's inconvenience. Of course, if any of you have any further issues, make the call to I.T. Don't come waste my time with crap I can't do anything about. And finally, you have all been emailed the quota for today, meet it."

Without another word, he strolls back to his office.

This is it.

I inhale sharply and get up from my chair.

"Make sure you come say bye when he's done firing you." Nicki says, with a half-hearted smile.

"I appreciate the encouragement." I say, shaking my head and walking away.

Time feels as though it has slowed as I cross the room toward his office. Everyone else is busying themselves at their desks and beginning to take calls.

Robotically, I force myself forward. Eight very stiff steps later, I am at the closed door of his office.

My legs feel numb as nerves flood throughout me. Gingerly, I knock on the glass of the door.

"What?" He snaps. Distracted by something on his phone. His greying hair sits perfectly in place, combed back with hair oil.

His pointed nose and wide chin stand out most when taking note of his features. Followed closely by his far too thick eyebrows and deeply wrinkled forehead.

I take one final steadying breath and open the door.

"I'm sorry to interrupt, Mr Yates. Do you have a moment to spare?" I ask, trying to keep the shakiness in my voice from becoming obvious.

He looks up from his phone, and his gaze immediately falls to my breasts. An icy shiver spreads throughout my veins. I clear my throat, trying to draw his attention away.

"Yeah, I can spare a minute. Actually, I could use your help with something." His voice is low, and his eyes darken.

"Sure," I say quietly. Knowing that if I want any chance of him saying yes, I need to say yes to *him*.

"Great." He tightens his hand around his phone and gets up from behind his desk. He strolls around to the other side of the desk and points to one of the two empty chairs, telling me to sit. I do as he instructs, keeping my eyes locked with his.

"I wonder, Miss Locket." He pauses, and I think he is just going to loosen his tie, but he removes it completely and drops it on his desk. His lips part just enough for the tip of his tongue to move slowly across his bottom lip.

My stomach flips, and bile rises up my throat. He unfastens the top button of his crisp white shirt, and wiry chest hairs poke through the opening.

I need to cut this short; it's time to get this over and done with.

"I need to take some time off, starting tomorrow. I apologise for the short notice, but something came up unexpectedly. I will be gone for two weeks. I respect that it is unprofessional of me to give such short notice, but could you please consider my request?"

There, I did it.

"Two weeks? With a single day's notice? Do you have any idea how far behind you will be on your quota, taking that much time without giving an appropriate amount of time for rescheduling?" He scoffs.

Here we go.

"I understand that this will create some issues, but I am asking you to please make an exception. I never take sick days, nor have I requested to take time off for personal reasons."

He steps away from his desk and closes the gap between us. Positioning himself close enough for the stink of cigarette smoke on his breath to burn the inside of my nose.

Reaching forward, he tucks some loose hair that had fallen out of my bun behind my ear. I shift in my seat and move my head away from his hand. He narrows his thick eyebrows, and his lips fall into a disapproving frown.

I knew this was coming, yet still, my eyes widen in shock long enough for them to begin drying.

Shit, I'm about to quit my job.

All of the air is sucked from my lungs as my mind races. His sharp gaze holds me in place, and my mouth falls slack, just barely enough to notice with words that sit on the very edge of my tongue but refuse to move past my lips. Hate-filled words about his inappropriate behaviour and his repulsive, thick, hot, smoke-filled breath.

"You know, Miss Locket, it wasn't easy to claw my way up the chain of command and end up where I am today. I had to do things I didn't like, I had to make sacrifices, and I had to push myself beyond the things I was comfortable doing. You are an asset to this company, and to me, but at this rate, you're going to be stuck out there behind that screen taking calls for idiots who don't know on from off. It's about time you started showing some real initiative. I think it's time you started letting me see how far I can push you beyond what you're comfortable with."

I gasp, loud enough for him to hear, and it pisses me off. First, because I really thought I could keep my resolve better than this, and second, because I knew to expect this, well, something like this to happen.

He is staring at me, his daring eyes sucking all of the air from my lungs until I feel deflated, fragile and painstakingly helpless. I don't dare move, I can't. Not when it feels like he's going to react to something as small as a position change. As if he is a lion waiting for the perfect moment to make the leap toward an already injured elk. His claws are at the ready to latch on tight and hold the elk in place in this god-forsaken chair.

"Well?" he asks, expecting the answer to a question I'm still not entirely sure he actually asked.

My lips part, and my breath catches in my throat at the shock of the sudden inhale I make, only just realising I had been holding my breath.

"You sick bastard." The words come out rushed and barely audible.

"Excuse me?" he arches his back and straightens his shoulders. "Go ahead, humour me, repeat what you just said."

Heat builds from somewhere deep inside. It spreads like wildfire, burning as it does. The pressure from the heat builds until I'm on the brink of cursing the uncomfortableness of it.

"I said you're a sick, perverted fucking pig, and I quit. Just as soon as I report you to HR."

The heat subsides with every word I spit at him, as if it were those words that had created the fire in the first place.

I wait for him to explode, for him to throw hurtful insults and powerful threats my way as I have heard him do from across the office on more than one occasion. But he doesn't yell, he doesn't even look affected by my words. He raises an eyebrow and leans back against the desk. He picks up his tie and, using his right hand, he wraps the tie around the left.

"Oh, how I would love to see you bound, gagged and taught some damn respect. You're a rather fit-looking thing, yeah, you'd have the energy to go a few rounds before becoming completely useless. That's plenty of time to teach you some fucking manners."

My mouth once again falls open on its own free will, and my eyes are wide. I struggle to collect my thoughts beyond *get out*.

"Did you not hear me? I'm going to report you. You're going to lose everything."

He laughs, a genuine, from-the-stomach laugh that sounds wrong coming from such a vile man.

"You're all the same, you come in, can't handle a little bit of a challenge and decide you have the power card because we have a HR board. Haven't you ever wondered why no one speaks up, Samantha? Why everyone either gives in to me or leaves?"

My name on his lips makes me want to heave. I don't give him the satisfaction of an answer. But he takes upon it upon himself to continue regardless.

"It's because they know it wouldn't matter. It *doesn't* matter. I hand-picked the whole HR team. Hell, I have golf with Marcus this Saturday. You report me, they take notes and pretend to care, then as soon as you leave the room feeling like you've done something for the women of this company and yourself, they run their notes through the shredder."

I don't give myself time to second-guess it. The burning in my throat has begun. I leap out of the chair and run straight for my desk. By the time I reach it hot tears are already rolling down my cheeks.

"How'd it go?"

I quickly glance at Nicki as I collect my things.

Her expression mimics what mine had just moments ago. Eyes wide and jaw hitting the floor.

"I'll see you around." I choke out through a half-arsed smile.

"Wait!" She calls out, throwing her headset onto the desk and getting up from her seat. I ignore her. I can't stay here, not for another second. Not at the risk of having to look at him again, no matter how much the sight of Nicki looking so desperate and miserable makes my chest tighten painfully. The elevator doors close, blocking my view. I slam the ground floor button and run my hands through my hair, pleading silently with the elevator to hurry the hell up. It finally opens, and I weave my way through the lobby, out the front doors and across the lot to my car. My stomach doesn't allow me the time to unlock it, before I get the chance to I am hunched over, my heart racing and my stomach contents now covering the small patch of ground below one of the hedges that line the outermost parts of the carpark.

Someone nearby mumbles something to someone. I don't catch most of it, but the words "gross" and "disgusting" are enough confirmation that they're talking about me. As if the universe has decided to slip me a favour, my stomach settles abruptly, and I manage to get myself and my things that I had dropped by the car inside.

I pull quickly out of the lot, my vision is blurred, my tears that stain my cheeks, and my mind is racing, full of flashes of his vile breath and sickening threats. I shouldn't be driving, but I can't go back to the car park I was in. Not if I hope to settle the violent pounding in my chest. I wipe my eyes and pull out onto the main road, following the flow of traffic in the general direction of my house while I try to collect myself and work out my next steps. I need a new job, sooner rather than later. I need to let my mum know, if she finds out I finally quit like she wanted and didn't bother to tell her, there will be heavier consequences than I am prepared to deal with right now. Not to mention my poor dad will never hear the end of her ranting about how I never tell her anything. It's not the first time I've accidentally made him endure her relentless ranting because of me. I won't put him through it again if I don't have to. I know I can't call her while my voice is so shaky. I will call her later; for now, a quick text will do. I give the command for my phone to type out a to-the-point message to my mother. '*I just quit my job, I'm fine, I will call you later tonight.*'

There, that's step one of whatever it is I'm supposed to do now done. Step two is going to be get the hell out of dodge. I will figure out the rest while I enjoy sipping drinks on the shore of some likely overcrowded beach.

Four

Thunder rumbles in the distance, and with it comes the threat of heavy rain that the blackened clouds look ready to dump out at any moment.

My front gate comes into view, and I ease off on the accelerator enough to safely turn into my driveway. Raindrops slowly but surely begin to cover the windscreen, and I take that as all the convincing I need to hurry up, get inside, get the kettle switched on, and be ready for this storm to kick in properly. Both the one in my head and the one that is seemingly trying to match my mood.

I make sure to put my phone in my bag, then get out of the car and jog to my front door. I look down into my bag to fish around for my keys, but before I reach in, I freeze, and all the air is sucked from my lungs. The *door is already open.*

I run over my morning; I was frantic because I was nervous about talking to Yates - I almost left the house keys on the hook, so I can't help but consider that it's possible for me to have left it open. I shake my head and with it, my anxiety - the best I can. And I open the door all the way, remaining cautious and quiet just in case the unlikely has happened and someone really is inside my home.

I step through the threshold, and with trembling hands, I urge myself to continue stepping forward through the entryway and into the living room. Nothing seems out of place, and my shoulders relax just a fraction at the realisation. I will my feet to continue on, this time with the intention of heading into the kitchen that is just off the living room. I ball my fists until my nails are accidentally digging into my palms, a hiss squeezes through my teeth in response to the sudden, unexpected pain, and I slap my hand against my mouth and hold my breath, waiting to see if the potential intruder heard me.

After waiting so long in the quiet for any signs of someone else being in the house, my ears start to ring. I muster enough courage to continue on into the kitchen.

I barely make it through the threshold when I notice someone sitting at the dining table that sits off to the side of my kitchen island.

The surprised scream is out of my mouth before I can consider what a horrifically awful idea screaming was.

The intruder, with sand-coloured hair that flows down to the middle of her back and a dress that looks out of place in this weather, reaches up quickly to take something out of her ears, then just as quickly she is on her feet facing me. Realisation crosses her face, and she bursts out laughing. It takes me a moment longer than her to process what's going on, but as soon as it clicks, and I recognise that it's Alisha standing in front of me laughing, I am very quickly joining her in laughter.

"What the hell is wrong with you, Sammie?" Alisha says with her hands resting on her knees.

"Me?" I reply, my laughter stopping abruptly.

"You're the one who's sitting at my dining table after leaving my front door open - making me think someone had broken in."

Alisha rolls her eyes and puts her hands on her hips. Her red lips purse as she shakes her head, and she reaches out her right hand. "Give me your phone."

Instinctively, I pull my bag closer to myself. "Why?"

"Because I want to show you why I nag so much about you never checking your phone. I sent you a message telling you to not freak out when you get home. I wanted to hang out and decided to meet you here so I can make sure you can't use some lame excuse to bail on me."

She reaches out her hand for my phone, then stops and instead moves my hair out of my face, and she frowns deeply.

"You've been crying. Wait, why are you home already?"

I step back from her touch and lower my gaze. I don't know why I suddenly feel so ashamed. She would be happy to know I quit. She's been wanting me to for months. But part of me wishes I had been strong enough to actually do something about Yates, so his disgusting behaviours could end with me. I quit, but that means nothing to him. He will just move on to the next one. My stomach churns at the thought of Nicki sitting in that same chair, being spoken to in the same way.

"Hey. Seriously Sam. What's happened?" Alisha persists.

"I quit my job." The words are barely a mumble, and I'm not sure if she even heard, but her immediate reaction is to wrap her arms around me. As soon as she does, the tears start again, and I sob into her shoulder.

"Did he touch you? I'll kill him."

I compose myself enough to give her a broken response.

"No, he just said awful things. I requested to leave, and the things he said were." I shake my head. "The things he said were foul. So I quit on the spot." I wait for her to say something about not standing up for myself, but she doesn't, even though part of me wishes she would, so someone is holding me accountable for not doing anything and being a coward.

"I'm so proud of you." She says gently and strokes my hair.

Her words take me by surprise. I want to tell her there is nothing to be proud of, but I have no energy left to muster any words through the crying.

I'm going to make you a tea, go sit down on the sofa, then we can just hang out, put on some crappy daytime TV until you feel ready enough to go shopping. Your flight leaves at one pm tomorrow, so we don't have a lot of time." She pauses for a moment before continuing. "Then maybe after we can go out for dinner and dancing, try to forget this whole day, then you can start this vacation feeling reset?" There is hope in her voice, and realisation sets in.

"That's why you were here in the first place, isn't it?" I ask and wave my hand towards her dress that clings snuggly to her body, showing off all the curves she would be hoping it to. Its length sits just below the bottom of her arse and her breast, and almost plunging out of the top. It's a deep purple with sparkles covering the entire thing that almost dance when the light hits them. She looks fantastic, as always. But she knows I would never say yes to an invitation like this. Even on a good day.

"Maybe." She says as she turns from me and makes her way to the kitchen, waving a dismissive hand as she goes.

I want to scream in frustration. I know it's a dramatic reaction to my best friend asking me to come hang out, well, in this case, more like backing me into a corner and attempting to force me to hang out by making me feel like I have no choice because she came over already ready to go and now also knows I have absolutely no other plans. But this is what it's always been like with Alisha, ever since we met back when we were sixteen and took a handful of elective classes together. Over the years I have questioned how our friendship has lasted the last eight years - our personalities have clashed at every turn but it's like something bigger than both of us continues to keep us together and keep me unconditionally loving her, even in the moments I wish she would understand that the last thing I want to do after a long week of work or when I'm feeling utterly beat down is to go out drinking and dancing, or worse, drive the hour and a half to the next town over that has a ridiculous array of club options to choose from. I have always respected that this is what works for her, but it's not what works for me.

"Okay, I'm going to need you to stop looking at me like that, because that's a look that tells me you are about to say no to going out with me and you are going to once again try to convince me that sitting by the fire and watching a movie is a much better idea and I'm going to need you to understand that I am already made up for outside." she waves her hand, gesturing at me. "And we only need a good thirty minutes for you to get ready too – if you let me help."

And there it is, proof of her master plan. I ready myself to protest, but before I get the chance, as if Mother Nature herself is on my side, another thunderclap hits directly overhead, this one makes the entire house shake, and Alisha immediately goes ghost-white, and her eyes widen.

"I'm not going out in this," I say and decide to make the tea myself that she offered.

Alisha gives a big, dramatic pout but doesn't continue to argue.

"Coffee or tea?" I ask as I flick the kettle on to boil.

"None," she slumps her shoulders. "Can I just borrow your phone to call a lift?"

I turn to her, surprised. "You're leaving, I thought you were going to stay for a while, then we would go shopping. Wait, you didn't drive yourself here." As soon as I ask the question, I realise that I should have noticed her car in my driveway.

"Hell no, I'm not going out just to have one of us stay sober. I planned this whole night, but apparently, this storm has other ideas." She sighs before continuing. "It's hard to believe, I know, but I think you're right. There is no sense in going out in this storm. I hoped it wouldn't dump its load until later in the night. But whatever."

I roll my eyes at her crude comment and point at my handbag on the counter. "My phone is in my bag. Go ahead. Or you could just spend the night?" I know it's an empty offer because she always declines, she hasn't stayed at my house since we were both still living at our parents' houses, and even then, she preferred that I stay with her.

"Wait," I say before she's finished reaching for my bag. "Why don't you have your phone on you?"

She rolls her eyes and pulls her phone out of her jacket pocket she had hung on the back of the seat. "I have it, I used it to text you, remember?" She makes a show of waving her phone around. "Messaging you was the last thing I was able to do before it died. I planned for it to die before we left here," she says in a matter-of-fact tone.

As if it's my first day of being her friend, I look up from the spoonful of coffee I opted for rather than tea that I'm about to dump in my mug and make the mistake of letting my curiosity get the better of me.

"Why would you purposefully make sure your phone is dying before going out drinking for the night?"

"To avoid drunk texting, duh." She responds without missing a beat.

"Does your own safety ever cross your mind when you are making decisions for moments like this?" I ask, already sure of the answer.

"Not particularly. I can hold my own." She shrugs, then holds my phone up to show that she is going to make a call.
"Put that down, just let me finish my coffee, and I will drop you off. I need to go shopping anyway.

Let's both ignore the fact that it's not even midday yet, so you aren't able to go out dancing for at least another six hours, maybe more. That's assuming you want to start your night early. You could, how-ever, go home, get changed and come shopping with me. I'm going to need your help." Now it's my turn to dramatically pout at her to get what I want.

Reluctantly, she agrees to my proposal, but as usual with Alisha, there are strings attached. I can see it coming before she says anything. She pauses for a moment, mulling over her compromise.

"Okay, let's do it. But I get to choose all of your clothes. Everything from a just-in-case raincoat to lingerie."

I cringe inwardly a little at the choice of the term lingerie over underwear, and I know it's not just be-cause it's her preferred term. This was a very on-purpose decision, and if she has it her way, I won't be going on this holiday with as much as a strip of cotton on anything. I can always just pack a few handfuls of comfy clothes and underwear into my luggage. It's not like she's going to know. Not until it's too late."

"Fine, if that's what it will take for you to come shopping with me instead of me coming clubbing with you. I will let you choose all my clothes."

She grins ear to ear, satisfied with her victory. I've already got some ideas that you will look so hot in. I'm going to make sure this is the best vacation you've ever had. And until I get there, I expect you to call me every morning with all the details from the night before because I promise you when I'm done with you, you're going to have sexy details to share." She flicks her hair back over her shoulder and picks my keys up from the counter.

"Hurry up and get changed. You've got me excited to leave now."

Five

The Uber into the city to get to the airport was a nightmare, between traffic and roadwork, I truly didn't think I would make it. I reach the terminal right as the final boarding call is being announced. I can hardly remember the last time I was inside the airport and got turned around three separate times. "I'm here, here's my ticket." I rush to the booth and shove the ticket at the flight attendant. I immediately feel rude and give her an embarrassed smile and apologise.

She tells me not to worry and ushers me through boarding bridge and onto the plane. The waiting flight attendant glances for just a moment at the boarding pass that I hand her and directs me to the left of the plane through a dividing curtain. I cuss out Alicia quietly to myself for spending the extra unnecessary money. Joke's on her, before this plane leaves the tarmac, there will be money in her account to replace the cost she paid for my ticket. It's going to start a whole drama that I almost consider not giving the time of day to. But I can't let myself enjoy the experience of first class, for the first time in my life, while my stomach is in a guilty knot, knowing she paid far too much.

As I walk down the aisle, I keep count of the seat numbers lining the overhead. I finally locate mine. The guilt in my stomach is replaced by a rare moment of excitement. I'm not just in first class for the first time, but I'm also the window seat. I step forward to get to my seat, but my leg hits something hard.

"Ouch. What the?"

I jump back, and that's when I see it, and my stomach immediately drops. My cheeks grow hot as I lock eyes with an impeccably dressed man. I can't recall a time I have ever seen a perfectly fitted suit before, but I'm sure I'm looking at it now. His white dress shirt is unbuttoned at the top, exposing a few chest hairs. His matching black jacket and trousers are perfectly in place. I have seen men wear suits every day of my working life, but never before have any of them looked like this. Neither of us breaks eye contact. The brown of his eyes is like dark topaz and has me suck in place. He shifts in his seat, moving from stretched out and comfortable to upright, it's still not enough for either of us to break away. I will myself to, it's a crazy thought, but it's almost as if he is challenging me to be the one to break. His stare is intrusive. It's making me feel naked, like not a thought is my own, and he can see right through me and what I'm thinking. My breath catches, it's only for a moment, but in that fraction of time, I feel like I'm drowning.

"Miss?" The flight attendant places her hand on my shoulder, and I startle. Finally breaking free of the hold he had on me. I turn to look at her, but not fast enough to miss the smirk that sits on the man's lips. I linger for just a little on the light stubble that lines his jawline, and my throat dries.
"Sorry, yeah, this man is in my seat." I hand her my boarding pass so she can see the man's mistake.

"I'm sorry for the mistake, Mr Truette. She says with a few flutters of her eyelids. I would roll my eyes, but it would make me a hypocrite and that happens to be my least Favorite personality trait.
"Ma'am, your seat is here, across the aisle." She points to the empty seat behind me, directly across from Mr Truette.
I stammer an embarrassed apology and take my seat in time for the seatbelt lights to come on. I fasten my seatbelt in place and scramble to find my phone

in my handbag. I throw a glance up at the steward-
ess who is now making her way back up he isle and
as fast I can before I get chewed out for using my
phone and draw any more attention to myself, I
open my bank app, scroll down until I see Alisha's
name and in a rush send her six hundred dollars, I
have no clue if it's no enough, or too much to replace the price of my ticket. I will find out when I
land and send her more if needed. For now, I angrily
type out a quick text.

Me: WTF is with this ticket???

and hit send, then put my phone on aeroplane
mode. Not so much because I'm pretty sure you're
supposed to, but mostly because I know she is going
to reply immediately, and I can't deal with that right
now.

"Anything I can get you, Mr Truette?" A different
flight attendant asks, this one has her chestnut hair
tied back into a neat bun and her smile is Hollywood
dazzling. I watch as discreetly as possible in such
close proximity at her twinkling eye and ever-rising
cheeks.

I snicker a little to myself, not because I'm judging her reaction, but because I now get to see how I looked just moments ago. Of course, I wasn't as put together as she is. In fact, the realisation that I haven't seen what I look like at all and can only assume I'm a standout mess compared to everyone else sitting around me because of the mad rush I was in to get here in time makes my snickering cut short. I find myself glancing at the man, only to catch him already looking at me.

"Two whiskeys, straight."

"Sir." The flight attendant says with a small nod of the head before moving on to the seat behind him.

I busy myself by looking through my bag for something to help with this ever-growing headache. Finally, I find some painkillers right at the bottom of my bag, they're the last two in the foil packet rather than in a box, and there isn't an expiry date in sight, but I decide to chance it anyway. I realise I have no water to take them with, just in time to see the flight attendant is already three rows further back.

I throw my head back against the seat and let out a defeated sigh. I am tempted to just throw them back without water, but that has never ended well for me in the past. I close my eyes and decide that perhaps the best choice for right now is to try to sleep for the next two hours away. It will mean sleeping away the expensive tickets, but at this point I couldn't possibly care less.

"Here." The man next to me says, and curiosity forces me to open my eyes.

He has his hand outstretched with a bottle of water. I hesitate for a moment. He is a complete stranger, and I have no clue where he has just pulled this water from. For all I know, he has added something to it, and I'm a convenient victim.

As if he senses my fear, he opens the bottle, I hear the seal crack, and he takes a drink from it. Keeping his eyes locked on me the whole time.

"Here." He repeats himself and holds the bottle out again.

"Thank you, Mr Truette." His name feels strange on my tongue. I play with the sound of it a little in my head. No, not strange, familiar. I've heard that name before. His left eyebrow raises slowly, and he tilts his head ever so slightly. God, I'm staring at him again. I offer a quick grateful smile as I take it from him and pop the two pills into my mouth, chasing them down with a too-big gulp of water.

"It's Alexander."

"Sorry, what's Alexander?" It's my turn to raise an eyebrow at him.

"My name. I'm Alexander Truette. There's no need to refer to me as Mr Truette. Unless, of course, you prefer that." He winks at me, I feel like there is some hidden joke sitting right behind his eyes that he is hoping for me to catch onto, but the only place my mind goes is somewhere too dirty to possibly say out loud.

I chuckle and shake my head a little disapprovingly, mostly at myself.

"This is normally the part when you tell me your name."

"Umm, it's Samantha, uh, Sam." I stumble. God, what is it with this man? Sure, I'm not usually known for having the strongest backbone, but never before have I felt so vulnerable when talking to someone. Even now, as his eyes bare into mine, heat rises from the forming knot in my stomach all the way to my face. It's distracting and making it feel impossible to string a cohesive thought together, let alone a sentence out loud.

"Do you happen to have a last name, or is your name Samantha Sam?"

I'm stuck on the flash of a perfect smile he gives; it makes my breath hitch for just a second.

"It's Locket, Samantha Locket. Like the Jewellery." I curse myself for saying more than just my name. I'm sure he doesn't need to know how to spell it, which is usually the only reason I ever add the thing about the jewellery.

He nods slowly and smiles just enough for the edges of his lips to curl. It's subtle, but for some reason I'm glad I didn't miss it.

"How fitting."

My mouth falls open like one of those terrifying clowns you're supposed to put balls into. Before I can say anything, the flight attendant returns and hands him both of his drinks.

Will there be anything else, Mr Truette?"

"No, that's fine, thank you." The flight attendant leaves once again. I sink back in my seat, annoyed that she had not yet checked if there was anything I want. I might be annoyed by the tickets, but I am here, so I might as well get full use of them, and right now I feel like something to eat and something nice and strong, preferably something that burns on the way down, is exactly what I need to distract from the man beside me and the chaos that is Alisha Quinn.

"Is something wrong?"

"No, nothing important," I reply, this time not looking over at him.

"Well, important or not, perhaps this will help heal whatever ails you." This time I can't help but look. How could I not when someone says such a ridiculous thing?

"What ails me? What century are you from?" I laugh, and he places down the glass of whiskey he had in his hand and dramatically holds his hand over his chest. "Alas, sometimes I find myself thinking I was born in the wrong one." I laugh more, and he picks the glass back up and hands it to me. Normally, I would be reluctant, but I take it from him right away and thank him. I bring it to my lips, the smell is divine, it's oaky with a hint of spice.

"Not yet." He says, before I can tip up the glass. "First, tell me why you are travelling."

"I hesitate at first, I know nothing about him and normally wouldn't feel comfortable sharing personal, well, anything about myself, but something feels different this time, and either way, once we get off this flight, chances are we are never going to see each other again, so screw it. Maybe talking about my chaotic last few days will help lift some of the mental load I have been carrying around because of it.

"My friend planned and booked a holiday for us both. Unfortunately, something came up at work, well, not unfortunately. It's an interview for a pro-motion she's been wanting for forever. But it means she has to join me in a few days rather than starting this holiday together. I normally don't do anything like this, but I just quit my job and decided I have nothing to lose right now, and it's the perfect time to try being a little spontaneous." I'm a little thrown off by him continuing to listen intently. There is no interrupting to say anything, just nodding every so often, like he is completely taking in every word I speak.

"What about you?" I ask, surprised that I genuinely want to know.

"I'm just getting back from some meetings in Melbourne, mundane stuff, I won't bore you with the details. I work for an international loans company, and I have some personal interest with the business wanting a loan through us."

I play around again with his name, and why on earth it sounds so familiar, I look at him and try so hard to place it. I go back over what he just said about Melbourne, and then it hits me like a wall of bricks tumbling around me.

"Truette as in Truette the bank?"

He sighs, and his shoulders drop. He seems to study me for a moment. It feels like he is trying to figure something out about me, but I can't for the life of me imagine what.

"You're quick with it, I'll give you that. Yes, Truette as in Truette bank."

He holds out his hand for me to shake. I feel awkward and awfully formal, but I oblige him. "Let me introduce myself again, correctly. "Alexander Truette. CEO of Truette holdings."

"Impressive." I say with a polite smile. He smiles a little, but it doesn't quite seem sincere. I remove my hand from his, and a somewhat awkward silence surrounds us. It's broken by his phone vibrating on the tray in front of him. He picks it up but immediately swipes it away. A vein forms in his neck, and I watch as he seems to ferociously type something on his phone. He finishes and puts it back down in front of him. And replaces it with the glass.

"To being spontaneous." He says and holds up his glass.

"To being spontaneous." I repeat and immediately down the whole thing, savouring the warmth of the burn in leaves on the back of my throat.

I thank him again for the drink and decide on turning my phone back on so I can read one of my eBooks. I steal another glance to my side while waiting for my phone to turn on, and Alexander is once again ferociously tapping away, seemingly messaging someone.

My phone finally turns on, and there is a message waiting for me from Alisha and two missed calls, one from her and one from mum. I type out a quick text to mum, letting her know I will call her later tonight and take a deep breath before opening the one from Alisha.

Alisha: Get over it. And I hope you know
That money will be back in your
Account before you land.

Drink as much as I would

And for the love of God

Let yourself have fun! Xx

I want to yell at her and hug her all at once. She's frustrating as all hell, but her heart is always the biggest in the room. She's right. I'm already here, I'm already doing this, and as much as I'm disgusted by the money she's spent, it's too late to do anything about it now. I will just use as much of my own savings money as I can while still making sure I leave enough for myself to get by until I can land another job when I get home.

A better, smarter idea than reading hits me. I close my messages, deciding to reply to Alisha later. I instead open my job search app. I spend the remainder of the flight updating my resume and applying for a handful of jobs that are available. There are some retail jobs, a cleaner position and a fast-food place. All options are completely different to what I'm used to, but right now that feels like a good thing.

I am vaguely aware of Alexander next to me, talking on the phone. His tone is reasonably hushed, and I catch only parts of the conversation.

"I know I should have pressed charges."

"She lives hours away; well, that's what she told me anyway."

"Yeah, yeah, I will keep my options open and let you know what I decide to do, but I really would prefer to just let things be."

The conversation shifts to planning a meetup for a round of golf in the next few weeks, and I tune out and get back to my job hunting. Stopping only when the announcement comes that we are approaching the city.

I gather my things and get ready to land. A small part of me is a little sad at the notion of my time in first class is over. *And my time with Mr Truette.* I'm being ridiculous.

The plane lands, and as it finishes taxiing, excitement for the unfamiliar, the new and the breath of fresh air for the next two weeks bubbles up.

"It was a pleasure to meet you." Alexander has his hand extended for me to shake again.

"It was a. I mean. It was nice to meet you, too." I curse under my breath for stumbling over my words.

Six

"This isn't real." I whisper to myself as I walk through the door of the hotel room, or hotel apartment, is more accurate. I drop my bag on the dining table and slowly cross the clean, white-walled room with beach-themed artwork to my right and large bed to my left with crisp white bedding towards the impossibly big windows and sliding door that opens up to a balcony that gives stunning views to the ocean below. The cloudless sky is a welcome sight compared to almost always overcast skies I'm used to back home. The beach is flooded with people. Families playing together, a group kicking a ball around, people swimming, and windsurfing.

For right now, I decide to allow myself to feel excited about this holiday, rather than just guilty that Alisha has used so much of her money to make it happen. I decide to begin enjoying this trip immediately. It's the late afternoon so by the time I have a shower, get changed and do my hair and makeup it will be time for dinner but rather than just going to find some cheap take out like I had originally planned I will instead take some money out of my savings and allow myself to eat downstairs at the restaurant and enjoy a drink or two.

I make quick work of my shower, washing away the day's travel. It's heavenly in the spacious two-person shower with beautiful water pressure and water that's on the brink of scalding. Very unlike my usual shower at home, which sits over a bath, has rattling pipes and the ability to provide what I compare to a light sun shower. Although the temperature of the water has always been perfect.

I wrap my hair and get started on my makeup. I decide to change it up from my usual light and natural and go a little bolder. I add a red lip instead of just gloss, a little blush to put a subtle colour to my cheeks, and a light contour. Just enough that it looks like I know what I'm doing, but secretly, I've never really been able to master it. It makes me wish Alisha were here. She would jump at the opportunity to be doing this for me, and although normally I fight her on it, I find myself desperately wishing for it now.

After giving my hair a blow dry and brush through, I do my best to get it to sit nicely over my shoulders, and I position my curtain bangs how I want them to sit. Once I'm satisfied that I have tied myself together the best I think I'm going to manage, I get started on working out what I want to wear to dinner. The shopping trip I let Alisha take me on was fairly successful, and truthfully, although I ended up buying some things I would typically find way out of my comfort zone, I actually ended up loving once trying them on.

I decide on a burgundy midi dress with a built-in corset and a slit that runs up my thigh. It was one of the ones I wasn't expecting to fall in love with once it was on, but it ended up hugging me everywhere I needed and make my breasts sit in a way I didn't know they could. I flick through the section of my suitcase that has my underwear and pick up a pair of black cotton panties. I hesitate for a moment and put them back down, instead picking up a black lace pair. I have no intention of letting anyone see them. It *would have been nice if Alexander had seen me like this.* Whoa, where the hell did that come from? I shove that dark, inappropriate thought way back down to whatever pit it crawled out from and make quick work of getting dressed, finishing the outfit off with some black heels. Once I'm done, I quickly move some money into my main account for dinner. I pass the full-length mirror on my way to the door and do one last check to make sure everything looks to be in order, and I haven't accidentally let my dress tuck into my underwear or have toilet paper stuck to my shoe. Something that would be just my luck to make me look as out of place in such a nice hotel as I already feel. I decide to take a quick photo of myself, it's rare to catch me in something that isn't work clothes or sweats of some sort, and I figure it's for the best to capture it.

I send it to Alisha with an accompanying text

Me: Going downstairs for dinner,
I'm going to find a way to return
That ticket money. Thought you
Might want proof I'm trying
To have fun. Xx

I hit send then remember I was supposed to also let my mother know I was here. I told her I would call, but I don't want to be stuck on the phone for the next hour, so instead I type out a quick message to let her know where I am and that I will call her sometime tomorrow.

With one last glance at myself in the mirror and a satisfied nod, I grab my purse and head to the elevator.

Once inside, I allow my mind to drift to Alexander. I allow it to remember the way his long fingers looked wrapped around the glass of whiskey and how hearing my name on his lips sounded made my stomach tighten just a little. The elevator doors open, and I realise that same tightening is happening again. I shake it off, broaden my shoulders and make my way through the lobby, exiting out to the street and into the adjoining restaurant. To my surprise, it's not overly busy, and the male server with a beautiful, friendly smile and scruffy, but tamed copper hair seats me almost immediately at a little two-person table by a window. He hands me a drinks menu and tells me he will be back in a moment to take my order and bring me a dining menu.

I scour the drinks, and it makes me frown. I don't recognise the name of most of them and once again feel out of place. I settle on a red wine with a name I can barely say. I know nothing about it beyond the menu having it in the red wine category, so I figure it's a safe bet in the hopes I can pair it with a pasta dish or steak. The server returns, and I place my order for wine and give the dining menu a browse. I decide to go with sweet potato fries and a rocket salad, then I find an eight-hour slow-cooked rib eye with seasoned vegetables and pepper sauce. My mouth immediately waters, confirming that it's what I'm ordering.

While waiting for the server to return, I take a sip of the wine. It's beautifully fruity and has a much bolder flavour than I was expecting. I take another appreciative sip, surprised by how much I'm enjoying it.

I find myself people watching, the window gives a pretty good street view of people finishing up at the beach as the sun just finishes setting, making the sky the most spectacular array of blue, purple and orange all melding into each other in a way I thought only a painter with exquisite talent could achieve.

A man comes into view, just the back of him, and he has already passed where I am sitting by the time I notice him. He has what looks to be a white button-up shirt on, charcoal trousers and what looks to be black dress shoes. I continue watching as he turns in towards the entrance of the restaurant. I can't help the curiosity and wait for him to come back into view once he enters the restaurant.

He steps through, and my stomach tightens, and my jaw is on the floor. Even from the side, I immediately recognise the light stubble, strong jaw, broad shoulders and brown eyes. The server gestures toward my direction, and I want to dive under the table. Part of me is practically giddy at the idea of seeing him again. I hate to admit it to myself, but he is definitely a specimen to enjoy looking at, and I found him interesting and educated enough during our conversations on the plane. It's a new feeling compared to my previous run-ins with men I had met back home. Some of them had been okay,

okay enough to give them a try for a few weeks, even less of them were okay enough to fool around with, but this is vastly different. The other part of me who is a coward and understands that we are very obviously from two very different world and social status's wants to run away and hide because I might be able to fake it in front of the server, hell I can fake it in front of every other patron in this restaurant but the way he bores his eyes into my soul like he can read every thought I have ever had makes me sure I could fake nothing in front of him.

He and the server walk right past me, and I let out a quiet "Thank god."

"Could you please just give me one second?" a familiar voice asks from only three feet or so behind me. I hear as he turns and walks back toward me.

Shit.

"Samantha?" he sounds surprised but also happy.

I take another quick sip of my wine before responding. "Alexander, what are the chances we would end up eating at the same place?"

He chuckles, and little smile lines form around his eyes. "I can tell you I certainly wasn't expecting it."

We are both silent for a moment, and I take another sip of wine in an attempt to calm my nerves, making themselves visible through my trembling hands.

"Are you waiting on someone?" I find myself unable to answer right away. I couldn't possibly be right, but he almost sounded like he was disappointed.

"No, just treating myself to a nice meal. I figured it was either this or take out, and I decided I would hate to waste this dress on a takeout place."

"No, that would be a shame indeed." His eyes darken as he speaks, and I watch as his eyes move from my face to as low as the table will allow and back up again.

"I don't suppose you want to join me?" I choke the words out before I can even process what I've done. It's a stupid request, and any notions I think he is putting forward are surely my imagination.

We are complete strangers; there's no way he would take me up on my offer.

"I would love to."

He excuses himself to the server and tells him he will be sitting at my table. He orders a drink without the menu, and the waiter tells him he will be right back with it and his dining menu.

Before he gets the chance to sit, I down the rest of my wine and repeatedly try to tell myself to relax.

"And another wine for Miss Locket, please." He says before the server has a chance to rush off.

"I don't have to join you if you're feeling in any way uncomfortable." He is smiling, but this time it doesn't reach his eyes, and his words feel empty. Like, he doesn't really mean what he is saying.

I mull it over, but it only takes a second for me to realise the sheer thought of him not joining me feels worse than the nerves.

"No, please. Sorry, it's just been a long day. That wine has had it coming since I ordered it." I joke in an attempt to make myself feel better and lighten the thick tension that feels like it's surrounding us.

His shoulders drop as if he has let out a breath he was holding, and he pulls out his chair and takes a seat.

"Have you eaten here before? Is the food any good?" I ask in a lame attempt at small talk, but also liking the opportunity to get to know him more.

"No, I haven't eaten here before. I'm staying in the attached hotel, so I figured it's convenient enough. I have some work to get done tonight, so I didn't want to go anywhere too far."

My mouth goes dry, and I find myself searching for the server, hoping to see him coming with my drink. To my dismay, he is nowhere to be seen, so I instead opt for pouring myself a glass of the table water I hadn't even previously noticed.

"You're staying here?" I say, to confirm, I heard what I know I already did.

"Why is that surprising? It seems like a nice enough place to stay."

"Oh, it's beautiful." I scoff. "Especially on the nineteenth floor," I respond after taking a gulp of water.

"You are staying here too?" he asks with an amused smile.

"It would seem so."

The server returns with our drinks, and the food menu for Alexander and I fight the urge to hug him. "I will give you a moment to look over the menu."

"That won't be necessary, I will just have the same as Miss Locket ordered." My stomach tightens at the sound of my name, and I quickly pick up the freshly poured wine and take a generous sip.

"Would you like me to ensure your meals come out together?"

Alexander starts shaking his head, but I stop him before he can do anything too polite, like say no.

"That would be perfect, thank you." Like hell am I eating by myself in front of him while he waits for his food.

A wicked smile crosses Alexander's face. "Actually, can you just leave the bottle and fetch another wine glass?" The server hesitates. "Sir, this bottle is three hundred dollars."

"That's no problem." Alexander says quickly.

"I will get you a fresh bottle." The server smiles and hurries off towards the bar.

"You know, big spending isn't something I'm easily impressed by." I confidently quip.

"No? Then please tell me, Miss Samantha Locket. What is it that does impress you?" His voice is low, and his eyes once again darken. Something about the way he says it makes it feel almost inappropriate, and I find myself ensuring no one hears the words that feel as though they were meant just for me.

"That's not something I typically divulge to a complete stranger."

"A fair answer, how about instead of that you tell me something you're interested in?"

The question stumps me more than it should. It's simple enough of a question, but for some reason, I find myself searching for something I should already know about myself. "Books, I'm interested in books." I finally respond.

"Reading or writing?"

"Definitely reading." I laugh to myself at the idea of me even considering writing. "How about you? What interests does a bank CEO have?"

He rests his elbows on the table and sits his head on his right hand, his index finger traces across the stubble on his chin, presumably in contemplation, but I fear even if he were to answer me right now, I wouldn't hear it. The sight of him damn near sucks all the noise from the room. I imagine what it would feel like to have his finger trace along parts of me instead, and my cheeks warm. A toothy grin flashes across his face, and it sucks all the air from my lungs.

Shit, did he notice me blushing? Surely it wasn't that obvious. I square my shoulders back, clear my throat and try to shove away my inappropriate thoughts.

Finally, he moves his hand from his chin, he leans back in his chair and runs a casual hand through his ink-black hair. It dishevels just enough to make some of the strands shift forward and frame a little of his face. My stomach immediately clenches, and a familiar heat threatens to rise from forbidden areas again. I pick up my wine and take a huge sip, two, three times in succession.

"My interests are quite typical. I too, enjoy reading. I find a lot of enjoyment in most physical activities. When I have the time for them, of course. I do, however, always make time at least once every three months to take the boat over to New Caledonia, or the plane. Weather and time of year, sometimes even just preference, depending." He shrugs and takes a sip of his wine that I hadn't noticed the server bring over as he said he would. Meanwhile, my jaw is on the table. It was obvious he had *some* money. I don't know enough about banks and how the CEO position works to know how much they make, let alone ones that are international. But boat and plane money? I squirm in my seat. I don't belong here, I don't belong in this restaurant or this nice hotel or sitting across from someone so incredibly out of my league.

"How much money do you have?" The words are choked out before I can catch them. My cheeks heat again, but this time for a very different reason. I will for the world to swallow me up on the spot and make it so I never have to be in the same city as this man ever again. This was a mistake, all of it.

I watch in horror as his eyes widen, and he seems to mull my question over. He is giving me nothing. I can't tell if he is pissed or disgusted. I search his face for anything. I lock eyes with him, and for the first time, I notice it. Tiny flecks of what looks like gold sit against the deep brown of his eyes. It's mesmerising. My thoughts are gone, my panic by some miracle is somehow replaced with pure awe. We hold each other in place. I feel every second go by as he, too, seemingly is searching for wordless answers from me.

"I am so sorry," I whisper. I don't mean for it, but it seems it's all I can manage. I'm the one to break contact first, and I look down at the napkin I'm fidgeting with in my hands.

"More than I have anything to do with." He finally puts me out of my misery. He sounds casual, like I just asked him if he likes the weather today.

"You don't have to give me an answer. That was completely inappropriate of me." This time I manage a little more volume, but I keep my head low. I can't bear to look at him.

He reaches across the table and places his hand under my chin. He tilts my head up and makes me meet his gaze.

"Don't, your question was surprising but fair. I do have expensive hobbies and tastes. It's no secret that I live a comfortable lifestyle. I just told you I sail and pilot planes. It's natural to be curious beyond that." His smile is warm and reassuring, but it's not doing much to help. Sail... Pilot. . . He never said...

"You didn't say *you* did those things." He seems to take a moment to figure out what I am saying before moving his hand and waving dismissively.

"Oh, I suppose you're right. I enjoy being the one in control, Miss Locket, not the one just along for the ride." He smirks.

Before I can say anything further, the server brings out the first of our food.

The server comes to take the last of our plates and the now empty second bottle of wine. My mind is buzzing, and I can feel myself swaying in my seat a little. I do my best to counter it and try to keep grounded. After the roller coaster of a dinner, this has already been I really don't need Alexander seeing noticing I *might* have drunk a little more than I probably should have.

"Tell me about your family." I find myself a little irrationally annoyed with him for somehow seeming perfectly sober compared to me.

"My Mum and Dad are retired and live a life split between their home and the van they travel around in. They typically aim to be home for six months and travel for the other." I finish up with a hiccup and naively hope he didn't notice. The quick flash of an amused grin tells me otherwise.

"That sounds wonderful." He sounds more like he is saying it to himself than to me.

"It seems to be, Dad makes it no secret that he would prefer to sell the house and travel full time, but Mum won't let them." The pang of guilt I've felt many times before when discussing this topic creeps in.

"What's stopping her?"

"Me. She never admits it out loud, but she doesn't have to. It's not hard to read the room when it comes to things like that, you know?" I'm fidgeting again, and the swirling in my head is becoming a little harder to fight against.

The server once again comes to our table. I notice for the first time how tired he looks. His hair is scruffier than earlier, and he has lost a little of his customer service spark.

"I am so sorry, but we are closing in fifteen minutes. Are you ready to pay the bill?"

"That's no problem, we are all done anyway." Alexander says as he pulls a card out of his wallet.

"No, you don't." I accidentally shout and hiccup again. "Technically, I invited you for dinner, so, Mr

Moneybags. I will be doing the well-mannered thing and paying."

"Would you mind, please, getting a glass of ice water before we leave?" The server nods and once again rushes off towards the bar.

"Now we can't have that. If you pay, then that would mean you're stripping me of doing the gentlemanly thing and paying for our first date."

My stomach flips over itself. "This was a date?" The question seems odd. Surely, I would know if I had been on a date. This was just two strangers making so they wouldn't have to eat dinner alone. No, not even that. This was just me being polite because I didn't know how to react when he noticed me. Right?

In my panic, I hadn't even noticed the server come back, and Alexander give him his card.

"It was if you want it to be." I am thrown by his nonchalant tone. Do I want this to have been a date? I think I would have much preferred to know that's what it was beforehand. Then again. Who says calling it a date has to mean anything more than that? I go on coffee and dinner dates with Alisha all the time. It never means anything. Hell, I've even grabbed lunch with a coworker before who I was joking with about it being a date. For all I know, Alexander is just being polite. We met today. We know the bare minimum about each other, the bare minimum for me being enough to know that I am intimidated, flustered, bewildered and confused all at once by this impossible man who I think I can allow myself to say I had one date with in a nice place while I looked nice and let it be an interesting story to tell Alisha when she finally gets here.

"Yeah, if you're okay with it." I do my best to match his nonchalant tone, but my drunken state betrays me, and I smile a stupid Cheshire-sized grin.

Seven

I catch a glimpse of us in the elevator mirror that lines the back wall. At first, I barely recognise myself. As bad as I'm feeling, I thankfully still look well enough put together. A little flushed looking, and my hair is still mostly in place, but it's the sight of us together that I can't peel my eyes from. Alexander is all broad shoulders, tall, perfectly put together, and to my utter shock, I look like I belong in the same world as him. I'm a complete phony, this outfit, this makeup, it's not the real me, but I can't deny that getting to play pretend for just one night has been fun and right now, standing next to Alexander, I can't help playing pretend just a little bit longer. Just until the end of the elevator ride.

"Which floor?" Alexander startles me out of my fun little fantasy of him and I together.

"Nineteen."

"What did you say?" His tone is amused, and it catches the entirety of my attention.

"I'm on floor nineteen." I pull my key card out of my bag to scan it, making it so the elevator allows us to go to my floor.

"There's no need for that." He taps his key card and presses floor nineteen."

"Wait, we're on the same floor?" I chuckle and once again hiccup.

"It would seem so." He seems distracted.

"This is turning out to be one hell of a coinci-dence," I say only somewhat jokingly.

Alexander's phone rings and he picks it up almost immediately.

"Truette."

I try to convince myself to not listen to a conversation that isn't mine, but the best I can do is pull out my phone and make it look like to him that I'm not.

"Well, that's just not going to cut it... No, I made it abundantly clear that I would not be able to reschedule again after this time. . . No, I don't want to drop them completely. It's not worth the paperwork. Just give them to Hanlen instead. I will no longer be collaborating personally with them. No, I will email her the details. No, that will be all for tonight. Turn the work phone off, Lauren. whatever comes in overnight will still be waiting for you in the morning."

The doors open, and he motions for me to get out first. I step out and look back at him. He offers a small smile, but it doesn't seem sincere. The exasperated hand he runs through his hair, although hot, seems to show his genuine emotion.

"Well, this is me." I say playfully as I step out the front of my door and ready my room key.

He glances to his left, and a concerned look washes over his face. It's gone as fast as it was there, and instead, his eyes are back on me. I watch as he trails from my eyes down as low as my navel, pausing on my breasts for a moment and back to my face. Is it possible he *wants* me? It's not, it can't be. Our worlds aren't made for each other. He has no idea who I really am. Who I am off that plane, out of this hotel? He is lusting after a lie.

"Thanks for the date. I was happy enough knowing I was going to be eating alone again, but I'm glad I didn't, I'm glad I spent it with you."

My brain and mouth lose connection again, and I'm saying it before I can stop.

"Technically, we can't call it a date yet." I glance at my room door and back at his enchanting gold-speckled eyes and down to his now slightly parted lips.

He figures out what I mean almost immediately, and in one swoop, I am pinned against the door, his hand is once again under my chin, the other around my lower back. He stares at me again, asking without words. I give a small nod, and its all the confirmation he needs. His mouth is on mine. He tastes of wine and smells so fucking good. He teases my bottom lip with his tongue, and I open a little wider, telling him to go ahead. We explore each other further. I drop everything in my hands and instead find the back of his head. I tangle my fingers in his hair and pull, just a little. He bites my bottom lip, and I involuntarily tilt my head back a little and moan.

"Fucking hell." He moans back against my mouth, and I pull him back in.

He releases his grip on me and takes a step back. I reluctantly let him. I fear that if I don't, I'm going to pass out from lack of oxygen.

"You. Are. Enchanting." His words come out in sharp bursts through each breath. It's nice to know it's not just me who was so affected.

"Come in with me." I whisper, I don't mean for it to sound like I'm almost pleading, but to my dismay, it does.

He takes a centring breath. "I'm not going to touch you in this state, Samantha. You've had far too much to drink."

I feel two feet tall. I jumped the gun. I let myself think he wanted me in that way, that's not what that kiss was. I can't help but feel like he is entertaining me because we ate dinner together and wants to be polite. I once again find myself unable to meet his gaze and instead follow down the length of his suit. *Oh?* He does want me like that. The evidence is clear in the now bulging seam of his trousers.

His phone rings once more, and I fight to rein in the disappointment.

"Thank you for tonight. Get some rest, you didn't end up drinking any of that water, and I'm sure because of that you're going to end up feeling like garbage."

To my surprise, he hangs up the phone.

"You didn't need to do that."

"Give me your phone."

I surprise the both of us when I pick it up, as well as my bag and room key from the floor, unlock it and hand it straight to him.

He presses a few keys and hands it back. "If you need anything throughout the night, for example, you think you're not okay because of the drinking, you call me."

His phone rings again, but this time he answers the phone and turns away from me.

I go inside as he says, but I decide against going straight to bed. I need a hot shower and to get this damn head spin under control.

***

I climb into bed feeling worse for wear. My head is pounding. The shower, although heavy, did nothing to help. I know any attempt to get to sleep right now will be futile. I contemplate having the TV on, like I normally would anyway, for the noise, but the idea of having a light that bright seems like a terrible idea. I decide instead to grab my phone off my

bedside table and check in with Alisha. I unlock the
screen to a new contact, Alexander. I hit the message button, and through blurred vision, I do my
best to type out a message.

Me: I hope you enjoy being right. My
head is pounding.
Thank you for tonight.

The reply is almost immediate, and I feel like a
giddy teenager excited that her crush is texting her.

Alexander: You know me so well
Already. I do enjoy
Knowing I'm right
But not at the expense
Of you.

I attempt to type a response, but I can't bear the
light of my phone screen any longer. I lock it and
put it back on the bedside table. With a groan, I roll

over and plant my face into the pillow and close my eyes as tightly as I can.

Minutes pass, two... five... ten. I can't tell, but the throbbing in my head is showing no signs of going anywhere.

A knock at the door startles me and makes my heart jump into my throat. I make my way out of bed and across the room pathetically slow. When I open the door, there is a member of hotel staff holding a tray with a glass of orange juice, an electrolyte drink and an unopened pack of ibuprofen.

I thank her and apologise for the inconvenience, feeling awkward that she has obviously had to run around and fetch these things and bring them to me.

I set the room lights to dim and put the tray down on the table, then waste no time taking the ibuprofen with the ice-cold orange juice. It tastes fresh, and it's heavenly. I finish the whole thing, then sit back down on the bed and sip at the electrolyte drink. Realisation hits me. Alexander must have called down to the lobby and asked them to do

this. As sweet as it is, I'm not sure I'm entirely comfortable with someone running around after me, let
alone at the request of someone else.

Me: That was incredibly
kind of you, but
unnecessary. There
was no need to have
someone run after me.

I lay back while waiting for his reply. I consider
the idea of looking Alexander up on the internet,
but I'm afraid I can't handle any more overwhelming new information about that man right now, and
instead let my eyelids drop as the headache slowly
but surely begins to fade.

Eight

I take a sip of the coffee I made, which happens to be surprisingly decent for hotel coffee and watch as the people below begin a mix of their morning work commute and enjoying the beach. I lean back in the beach chair and close my eyes. I get enthralled in the bustling sounds of the city and the waves below. My eyelids get heavy, and I allow myself to drift off, being mindful of the coffee in my hand. A knock at the door makes my nap short-lived. I contemplate ignoring it, finding the motivation to move from this chair feels damn near impossible, but then there is another knock. I admit defeat and reluctantly go back inside to see who it is.

A different hotel worker greets me with a friendly good morning and a hope that I am feeling better. It strikes me that she would even know I was feeling unwell. Perhaps she was also working last night? Or the other worker gave her a heads up? She is standing with a trolley full to the brim with break-fast foods. I hadn't considered that the room might have come with a breakfast package, but I'm not surprised, given how much I'm sure it cost.

I move to the side to allow her to come in with the trolley.

"Are you needing anything turned around in your room, Miss Locket? I will let housekeeping know."

"No, everything is perfect for now, thank you though."

"Please call down to the front desk if you're needing anything else."

"I will, thank you so much."

She leaves the room, and I look over the overabundance of food. There is toast, fresh fruit, muffins, scrambled eggs, bacon, and French toast. Various sauces and syrups. Two coffees with beautiful leaf designs on top, a teapot filled with hot water and the tea bags on the side. I'm never going to be able to finish alone. Another pang of guilt climbs claws its way into my chest. I'm not supposed to be eating it alone. I grab my phone. Alisha isn't here to *actually* eat it with me, but she definitely needs to see what she is missing. I take a photo of the food and go to send it to Alisha, but before I do, I notice some unread messages from Alexander. The first is him replying to me last night.

Alexander: Please get some rest.
I would love for you
to join me for dinner
Again, tomorrow night.

I find meals shared with
You are quite stimulating ;)

A Cheshire grin threatens to split my face in two. He wants to see me again. A familiar, too-loud voice echoes teasingly around my mind. *He doesn't want to see you, though. He doesn't have a clue who you really are.* I want to tell the poisonous voice to shut up, but the truth is, I know damn well my intuition is right. The person he met last night is a fake. He got a glimpse through the charade on the plane, but I can't help but to feel the version of me from last night is the one who caught his attention. And soon enough, if I were to try to keep up this charade, the cracks will show, and he will know who I really am. With a now deflated ego, I read over the second text.

Alexander: Good morning, I'm hoping
No reply means you fell asleep.
I'm not sure what you like for
Breakfast, so I just got a little

Of everything. Let me know about
Tonight. I will be anxiously
awaiting your response.

He did this. I once again look over the food, and that stupid face-splitting grin is back. I read the message again, and then again. He is waiting to hear from me; he wants to go for dinner again. He had the hotel staff run around for me twice now, with no expectation back from me. I roll my bottom lip between my fingers; I'm overthinking this whole thing. I'm only here for a little while. After I go home, I never have to see him again. While I'm here, I can be whoever I want. Who cares if I spend my time while I'm here in nice clothes, eating at places a little nicer than normal, within my limit of spending of course. Who does it hurt if, for the next two weeks, I have a temporary rebrand of myself, and Samantha Locket is someone who wears her head high on her shoulders and is spontaneous, rather than a work, home, read, repeat kind of person.

I get a wicked idea, and before I can change my own mind, I shimmy out of my pink cotton shirt and shorts pyjamas with daisies all over them and replace them with a matching lace black undies and bra combination. The bra is a push-up, and even I stop and linger for a minute when I see myself in the mirror. I give my hair a quick brush through, just enough to tame it into submission, then I move the coffee and tea to the side and, ever so carefully, grab the tray full of plates of food and put it on the bed. I position myself, so I am sitting against the bed head, cross-legged and pick up a piece of the buttered toast. I put the corner of it in my mouth and take a photo of myself. I don't even let myself look at it properly, knowing if I do, I will psyche myself out of it and hit send before immediately typing out a reply.

Me: Thanks for breakfast
That was really sweet
And unnecessary of you.
I would love to join you for

Dinner, but only if you help me through
Breakfast first. This is far too much.

I take a bite of the toast while waiting for his response. Anxiety fills my stomach at the realisation
of what I've just done hits me. I can't remember the
last time I send a photo like that of myself to someone, let alone after meeting them just hours ago. My
heart begins to thump harder as the panic rises. I
don't have to worry about being fake anymore because he is going to see what I have done and decide
I'm far too willing to put it out there.

I scramble to see if I can delete the messages before he sees them, if that's even possible, but as I'm
trying to figure it out, he replies.

Alexander: Delicious.
I will be right over. I will
 need you to put something else
On though, or I'm afraid it won't be food
I'm hungry for.

I nearly knock the whole tray off the bed as I leap off it and rush across the room to put the hotel-provided robe on. I tighten the belt into a knot and put the tray on the dining table.

Stop panicking, I repeat over and over. I asked him to come over. I need to get a grip. I re-read the text, and my stomach clenches. Heat rises to my cheeks, and I find myself picturing him on his knees in front of me. My fingers tangling in his hair to hold him in place.

A knock at the door rips me out of my daydream. I clear my throat and take a mouthful of the electrolyte drink from last night before opening the door.

Alexander is standing back from the doorway, and instead, in the hall, he is on the phone to someone, but even if I wanted to know what he was talking about, I'm sure I couldn't hear. There are no thoughts in my mind besides the grey sweatpants hanging for his hips in *that* way. His white V-neck tee clings to him, and sweat lines the top of his chest and back. How is it possible that even after he has clearly been working out, he looks magazine cover-ready? If I wasn't enjoying the sight of him, I would be pissed about the unfairness.

He smiles apologetically, and I shake my head to let him know it's okay. The longer I get to leer at him, the better. I watch patiently as he runs his hand through his hair.

"I don't care, just get it done. She is finding out everything somehow, and I ridiculous that no one has figured out how." Holy shit, that sounds serious. "I think we need to consider the possibility that someone is leaking information from the inside. I want everyone's accounts looked into, even Lauren's."

That sounds serious.

"Just their business accounts for now. It's all we legally can do. Do what needs to be done if we find nothing there."

He hangs up without another word and gives me an apologetic smile that quickly turns into a tooth-bearing grin.

"I see you did as you were told." He motions to my gown, and my legs threaten to give out from under me. He makes me feel utterly disarmed under the hold of his gaze.

"Well, we can't have you skipping breakfast, especially after you paid for it." His face falls, and his eyebrows pinch in the middle. "Is that why you asked me to join you? Because I paid for it?"

I'm taken aback by what sounds like disappointment. "Part of the reason," I admit. "But also, because you didn't have to go out of your way last night to eat with me, or get things sent to my room to make me feel better, or order me breakfast or. . ." He shakes his head and rubs his hand through his hair in the way that makes me jealous that it's not me doing it.

I thought it was because of what I was saying but he is once again pulling his phone out of his pocket and typing furiously.

"I'm sorry. There is something I need to take care of. I will be back in a minute to join you for breakfast." I do my best to hide my disappointment and give him a small smile.

"No problem, do whatever you need to."

He heads left, towards the room door next to mine and stops before it. There is a man I hadn't noticed before standing in front of it with a black suit, white button-down and black tie. His black hair is buzz-cut, and his square face looks focused on nothing but Alexander. What looks like an ear-piece sits in his right ear. He removes it as Alexander begins saying something I can't make out through their hushed tones. The man with the buzzcut nods his head towards me, but his expression remains hard. Alexander looks my way, and I realise this was very obviously a conversation that is none of my business.

I turn back into my room, closing the door behind me and decide that rather than dwell too much on whatever the hell that was, I will instead finish my now probably cold coffee on the balcony.

***

My phone dings, and I expect to see a message from Alisha, but instead it is once again Alexander.

Alexander: I apologise for before.
I am all finished up
If you would still
Like to share breakfast?

I toy with the idea of telling him something has come up. My insecurities are on display front and centre again and are the louder voice right now than the confident me I was just twenty minutes ago. I even get as far as typing the message out, telling him I can't, but just as quickly, I erase it and instead tell him I would still like to share breakfast.

Seconds later, he once again knocks. Was he already standing outside my door? He has changed out of his sweats and into navy blue trousers and a white button-down, but he has left the top open. I fear if I linger any longer, I'm going to start drooling.

"Come, come in." I stammer and move to the side of the doorway. "Join me while I finish my coffee outside."

"Yes, ma'am." His smile makes my breath catch in my throat.

He follows me out onto the balcony and takes a seat on the adjoining chair. We sit in a comfortable silence for a few minutes as I slowly sip at the last half of my remaining coffee.

"I'm sorry again for earlier." His voice is low, and he keeps his eyes fixed forward.

"There's no need for that. I can't imagine how busy you are. I would be more surprised if your phone didn't constantly go off." He chuckles a little, but it feels forced. "Who was that guy you were talking to, though?"

"My driver." Once again, his nonchalant answer has my jaw on the floor. I don't think I have ever come across anyone who has had their own driver.

"Oh." Is all I manage. *You're out of your league, Locket,* the voice in my head taunts. I put my cup down and get up from the chair. I rest my arms across the balcony and let the breeze rolling in from the ocean caress my skin. The smell of salty air fills the space around me, and I breathe it in, attempting to ground myself. I hate this. Never before have I had advances put forward by someone who even comes close to him in any way. He has been more thoughtful in two days than anyone I've been with for months. He has more money than sense and could have anyone who throws themselves at him, and yet he is here, sitting on my hotel room balcony, asking me to join him for breakfast and later dinner.

"Is everything alright, Samantha?" I hadn't noticed him coming up behind me. He stands beside me and places his hand at the small of my back. I take another breath and let myself lean into him. The warmth of his breath tickles my ear.

"Breakfast is going to be cold." I murmur.

"I apologise. Please, excuse me for one moment." He steps away once more, and the absence of his hand on my back is heavy, but he doesn't leave the balcony.

"I need another breakfast brought to Samantha Locket's room on the nineteenth floor... just some of everything again... the majority of the food is untouched, just cold. Please have housekeeping wrap it up. I will then have someone come to collect it." He hangs up the phone, and without missing a beat, he calls someone else. "Logan, in around thirty minutes, I need you to collect some food I am having packaged by the hotel staff. There was a woman we passed last night two streets over. . . yes, that's the one. . . If she is still there, I want it given to her. . . yes, I want it all given to her. That's all for now."

He hangs up, but this time puts his phone away, and he comes to stand back beside me.

"Has anyone ever told you you're incredibly bossy?" I glance up at him, and he is already looking down at me.

"Not if they want to keep their job." He winks, and I shake my head at him.

"Are you trying to impress me, Mr Truette?"

"Like that? No. You strike me as someone who doesn't swoon at the sight of money spent and highhandedness, but I *could* impress you, if you'd like."

I turn to face him, and his waiting gaze is darkened. Brown and gold meld with green. The air is thick with unspoken desire and the game between us begins. A battle of who is going to break the tension and decide to finally be bold enough to do something about it or put an end to it. I watch as his shoulders rise and fall ever so slightly faster and his lip's part just a little. Just like last night when - *Fuck it.*

"You've got me intrigued, Mr Truette." I whisper.

All amusement is gone from his face. It's my turn for my heart to drum violently. He loosens his tie as he steps toward me, closing the space between us. The world below us disappears and all that exists is Alexander. He removes his tie completely. "Hands." I do as I'm told and watch as he fastens the tie around my wrists.

"I need you to tell me this is what you want. I need to hear you say it." He tucks the hair behind my ear on the left side.

"I want you, Alexander."

He cups his hand behind the back of my head, letting his fingers tangle in my hair. He pulls me up to meet his lips, and I'm immediately lost in him. In the smell of his soap, the feel of his tongue playfully teasing my bottom lip, in the sound of the low guttural moan he lets out when I deepen the kiss to meet his desires. He tilts my head to the right and begins trailing light, soft kisses along my jaw down to my throat. My head rolls back, exposing more of my throat, and he continues his journey, kissing, sucking and licking down to my collarbone.

It's hot, it's overwhelming, it's outside!

I don't want him to stop. I consider how bad it would be if we did just stay right here. I could lean over the balcony, and he could take me from behind. If I keep my robe on and just lift it — no, that's not going to work. I need to see him. If I don't, I don't think I will believe this is *actually* happening.

"Take me inside, Alexander." I'm pleading with him again, and I don't even care. Every part of me is on fire under his touch, and I need more. I need him to touch me properly, everywhere. I need release from the building heat rising from the absolute depths of somewhere unspoken within.

He scoops me up faster than I have time to process, and it makes me squeal and giggle.

He puts me down at the foot of the bed. "Are you sure about this Samantha?" His words carry so much hope, and I waste no time keeping him wondering. Awkwardly, with my restraints, I untie the rope on my robe and let it fall open.

"Fuck." His words are sharp, and, in a flash, he is on his knees in front of me. My hands find his head just like I imagined they would earlier, and I playfully let my fingers tangle in it as he leisurely trails light kisses from my knee up the inside of my thigh. He runs his nose along the front of my underwear, but all too soon, he moves up to my lower stomach and continues softly kissing along the band of my underwear while running his fingers up the back of my right leg. He follows the line of my underwear along my arse at a torturous pace, then follows with the other leg, doing the exact same thing until both hands are cradling my hips.

He looks up at me, and I nod. "Please." I whisper, managing nothing more. He hooks his thumbs in my underwear and pulls them down. They fall down around my ankles, and I step out of them, supporting myself with my hands on his head.

He kisses me two, three more times. Then his mouth is on me. His tongue immediately circling my clit over and over, breaking only to occasionally suck and bite instead.

"Alexander" His name is a broken moan, and he swears again at the sound of it.

He runs his fingers up my leg again, and the mixing of sensations is almost overwhelming. I think he is going to trace around my arse again, but before I can think more on it, two of them are inside me. Torturously slow at first, and I move my hips, trying to encourage him to give me more. It's over before it's barely begun. He removes his fingers and stands. He glances down at his glistening fingers, and I watch as I realise he is going to put them in his mouth. I grab his hand and, ever so slowly, while looking up at him through my lashes, trail my tongue from his knuckle to his fingertip, then suck them both down. His breath catches, and I remove his fingers from my mouth with a satisfied grin.

"You don't play fair, Miss Locket." His voice is low and thick with desire. He unties my wrists, then slides the gown I am still wearing off my shoulders and makes it fall to the floor before taking a step back. He hungrily looks me up and down, and my insecurities threaten to creep back in.

"Enchanting." He whispers and once again comes closer. He traces his fingers along either side of my body. Stopping and starting again every time, he reaches the middle of my ribs and my hips. The sensation sends shivers of heat all through me, and I grow more and more impatient. The buildup is becoming too much, I want to scream at him to touch me properly, to get back on his knees *anything*.

His phone buzzes in his pocket. His hands are still in place on my hips, and he smirks. He pulls the phone from his pocket and brings it to his ear.

"Thanks." Is all he says, then hangs up the phone and puts it back in his pocket.

What the hell was that? I'm standing in front of him, almost completely naked, wanting him so bad it almost hurts, and he needed to answer the phone now to say thanks?

"Hungry?" His voice is low, and he pulls me into another kiss.

"Starving." I respond when he pulls away far too soon.

"Good, because breakfast is about to be here, and you need to eat."

"You're serious?"

He is already fastening his tie back into place.

"I'm sure. You might want to get dressed, unless of course you want the housekeeper to see you naked." He winks.

He doesn't want you. This time, I don't fight my subconscious into submission. I've never been so humiliated. I watch him head to the room door, and I will my feet to move. I want to scream at him, hit him, show him how fucked up and used he has made me feel, but my legs are concrete, and all I can manage to do is reach down for my robe and fasten it back in place. My throat burns as tears threaten to fall over the edge of my eyes. This is ridiculous. I can't remember the last time I cried over a guy. A *real* guy anyway. There are voices coming from the hall. I can't quite make out what they are saying, but one of them is definitely Alexander.

I step back until I feel the bed behind me and drop down onto it. I wrap my arms tightly around myself and try to find it in me to build up the courage to even be able to look at Alexander again.

He enters the room again with a different hotel room service woman. Her cheeks are flushed, and she seems a little unsteady on her feet. A little petty part of me wants to warn her away from him, but instead, all I manage is a polite thank you smile as she swaps the old breakfast trolley out with the new one. The room fills once more with the smell of hot toast, coffee and muffins. My stomach rumbles to my absolute horror, and I glance up at Alexander, who is carrying the tray of food over to the table. He is facing away from me and across the other side of the room, so thankfully didn't notice the evidence of my hunger, though I can't see how I can bring myself to eat. My stomach may be empty, but right now I feel the complete opposite of hungry. In fact, the knotting and churning as I try once more to build an ounce of courage back up is making me want to throw up.

Alexander turns back from the table after placing the tray down. He reaches for the coffee and looks up at me, smile on his face.

"Join me for breakfast, Miss. Oh? Oh shit." He immediately puts them back down and rushes over to the foot of the bed. He drops down onto his knees at my feet and grabs hold of my hands.

"Shit, Samantha, I'm so sorry. I..."

Is he seriously about to tell me he didn't mean to leave me standing in a heaping pile of self-consciousness and doubt? What the hell did he expect?

"I think you need to go." My voice betrays me. My words choke out as a tear breaks the surface and rolls down my cheek.

"Please, let me explain. I fucked up. This, this was never meant to happen."

The man I have gotten to know over the last day doesn't exist right now. He has been replaced by someone so profoundly sad and desperate. In what world should he be begging at my feet for me to forgive him? I'm a blimp of time in his life that he never has to think of again and can move right on to the next one. It doesn't make any sense for him to be looking at me with such misery.

"There is nothing to explain, Alaxander, you don't owe me anything. I misread the situation, obviously. I thought you wanted me in the same way I wanted you. It's not a big deal." I try for a dismissive shrug, but its half arsed.

"God, Samantha." He lets go of my hands and runs his hands through his hair. His phone begins going off again in his pocket. "Shit."

"Do what you need to do." I manage a small smile.

He pulls the phone out of his pocket, and I go to get up to get myself a drink. He swipes away the call and tosses his phone to the side.

"Just go, Alexander, we don't need to keep playing whatever fucked up game this is. Take your food with you, I'm not hungry." I wave towards the table. I wipe away a stray tear with the sleeve of my robe and get up from the bed.

"Samantha."

I can't deal with this right now. I don't want to look at him, I don't want to hear what he has to say. It would have been the easiest thing in the world to have never acknowledged me, it would have been easy to decline my offer at dinner, it would have been easy to not kiss my after dinner or come to my room this morning and keep up this fucked up confusing charade.

He doesn't move; he just runs his hands in his hair again in that way that ten minutes ago would have me on my knees in front of him.

"Samantha, please."

"Enough!" I shout. "Stop pretending you owe me anything. You don't need to apologise, and you don't need to pretend this is anything more than entertainment. You aren't interested in me; you've made that *very* clear."

His hands drop from his hair, and he grabs me by the hand once again. I try to move away, but he pulls lightly, urging me to stay.

"I'm not pretending." It's his turn to be vulnerable. His expression almost mirrors mine. His eyebrows are pinching in, and he looks lost, so very lost.

"Then what the hell was that? If that was your idea of being funny, clearly it didn't work." I shout.

"No, of course not. There is nothing funny about what I did. There's nothing funny about any of this."

"Then why, Alexander? Why did you join me for dinner? Why did you kiss me? Why did you act like you wanted more? Why the fuck are you here?" I'm shouting, and with every word, I watch as his face twists more and more into a broken mess of itself.

"Because I'm mesmerised by you, Samantha." He barely managed to whisper the words as he drops his gaze. "And for that, I am so sorry."

Five words are all it takes for me to buckle under him. If he wasn't holding my hands, I'm not sure I would believe the earth was still spinning below me. I shake my hand loose of his and hold it against his cheek. He places his hand over mine and leans his face into it.

"You can't be. We met a day ago. You know nothing about me. This is insane, Alexander. I'm nothing more than a casual fuck. Well, apparently, not even that."

He winces at my words but quickly recovers. He shakes his head and gives me a weak smile.

"Maybe, but I know you're feeling it too, and I know enough about you. I know the person you are pretending to be isn't the real you. I know this hotel, dinner, and your bold behaviour isn't how you usually are."

"How could you possibly know that?" My voice is meek, and I raise my eyebrow at him.

"You don't hide it as well as you think." He smirks at me, and my cheeks pink, giving him the confirmation he didn't need.

"Is that what's stopping you?" my voice is regretfully filled with sadness.

"No, Samantha, I am not that shallow. It has nothing to do with you, or who you are." He pauses and grabs the back of his neck. He rubs it and looks around the room, seemingly searching for the strength to find what he needs to say.

"I have some shit going on. Shit that honestly has me pretty fucked up. I want you, Samantha, more than I've ever wanted anyone. In your presence, the world seemingly stops. For just a moment, you make me forget. It's selfish of me to let you in when my needs from you are selfish, but I don't think I have it in me to stay away."

Holy shit. There's so much to unpack. He really does feel the same way. It's still hard to wrap my head around. This kind of thing doesn't happen in real life. People don't really lock eyes from across the room and then boom, happily ever after.

"Say something." He pleads.

"Be selfish," I whisper, looking up at him through my lashes.

"Samantha, you don't know what you're saying."

I go to argue back, to tell him I don't care, but I don't get the chance.

He lowers his hand from his neck and clears the three steps between us. All the oxygen is sucked from my lungs as I watch his eyes darken. In just moments, he has switched from defeated and miserable to looking like he is going to do unspeakable, sexy things that I wouldn't dare say out loud.

His hand is on the ball of my lower back, the other under my chin. He tilts my chin up, and in an instant, our lips are colliding. It's intense, full of desire and need, it borders on painful, but I don't care. My hands find his hair, and I firmly hold him in place. The world once again stills around us. Desire builds deep in my belly and there... *oh*, I need this man, now. I move my hand down his body until I find the front of his pants. Before I can start working on his belt, he pulls away.

"Not yet," he growls, and my stomach tightens more.

"You can't be serious."

"There are things I want to do with you, God, so many things. I need your strength for all of them. And I'm not letting another breakfast go to waste."

Damn this man. How can something as simple as the words he says have me feeling like I'm going to buckle at the knees?

I don't want to ruin what we've just repaired, and I seem to have finally found my appetite, so I begrudgingly agree.

Nine

My calves are burning, and sweat beads roll down every inch of my skin. With every painful step pounding the pavement, I will myself to keep going. It's been months since I've used a run to clear my head, and when I decided after Alexander left this morning, abruptly after a phone call, I had imagined it feeling a lot better than this. Every muscle in me is screaming to stop, or at the least slow off, but

I can't yet. In one morning, I have gone from he doesn't like me to holy shit, I think he likes me more than just a casual fling. His words circle around my mind.

There are things I want to do with you, God, so many things. I need your strength for all of them.

"I have some shit going on. Shit that honestly has me pretty fucked up. I want you, Samantha, more than I've ever wanted anyone.

I have no idea what he means by needing my strength, but holy fuck I want to know, but then I have so much I need to worry about, finding a job to go home to, being a big screaming priority. Perhaps I should heed his warning. He told me he has shit going on. I know nothing about the work he does or his family. Whatever he has going on could be anything, and I really don't have it in me to add to my plate right now.

I push forward, weaving in and out of people along the esplanade. I try to shake out the images behind my eyes of brown, gold-flecked eyes. Of my fingers tangled in his hair, of his mouth *there*. I need to call Alisha and tell her about Alexander. I already know she's going to tell me to stop overthinking it and enjoy it. It only has to last the holiday, then I can forget. . .

I buckle over, and the contents of my breakfast are on the pavement in front of me. *None of it has mattered.* Him being on his knees, holding my hands with such hope, me working out what the fuck I'm supposed to do. It's all been for nothing. We have two weeks. After that, it will be like none of this ever happened.

"Ugh, gross." A disgusted voice hits me straight in the gut as he walks past, and I vomit again.

I wipe my mouth on my sleeve, and with no idea what else I'm supposed to do now, I run back to the hotel, praying that I didn't get any on myself and can make it through the lobby and into the elevator without reeking of vomit.

The elevator door opens to my floor, and I walk the few steps to my door when a movement to the left catches my eye. Alexander's driver is standing out the front of the door next to mine again. Perhaps he is back from the office? Wait, is he standing out the front of that door because Alexander is staying in the room right next door? Why would he not tell me that? No, I don't care. I can't deal with any of that right now. I just want a shower and to call Alisha.

He notices me staring, and I smile at him. My cheeks pink with embarrassment at once again getting caught. His lips remain in a tight straight line, giving nothing away. I open my door and let myself in, but I can't help but notice Mister No Emotion pulls his phone out and type something. I consider the idea that he is letting Alexander know I am here, but it's a ridiculous thought.

I waste no time stripping from my vomit and sweat-covered clothes and getting in the shower. I turn the hot tap all the way up, and the cold just barely enough to take the edge off. The sting is heaven against my skin. I use the hotel-provided soap, thankfully, a wonderful vanilla scent, and it lathers beautifully. I make quick work of washing myself down, but allow myself to stay under the stream of water for much longer. I lose track of time.

My fingertips wrinkle and begin to sting, so I decide it's time to call the shower done. I make quick work of brushing my teeth and doing a mouthwash rinse to get rid of the horrible taste in my mouth.

I type out a quick message to Alisha, but before hitting send, erase it and decide to call her instead. It rings out, but it's not unusual for her to not pick up right away, so I try again, but it's no use. I sit down on the end of the bed, not caring that all I'm wearing is a towel, and I haven't even wrapped my hair, so it's dripping all down my back and making the bedding wet.

I trace my hands over the blanket. This isn't normal. There must have been something wrong with breakfast. My reaction to realising my time with Alexander is short was a complete overreaction. I won't allow myself to consider it being why I was sick. But as visions of him cross my mind once more. Not of him on his knees, making my head roll back or of him tying my wrists and single-handedly doing the hottest thing I have ever experienced. No, instead it's him sitting across from me at dinner discussing work, it's of him on the plane offering me his water and of him sending the hotel staff running around after me. It might have been an overreaction, but reality shatters around me. It was because of him. He might have been able to admit to me that he is mesmerised by me, but I'm not sure I can even admit to myself that I am mesmerised by him right back. How could I not be? In what world would a CEO bachelor who pilots planes, sails boats, has an unimaginable amount of money and looks like that, want me? I work, read, and on a good day, remember to feed myself more than one meal a day. I have nothing to offer him, at least not the real me, or even the fake me. I'm still the same person as usual, just shiny and able to look the part.

My ringing phone pulls me out of my spiral. I answer without even looking properly, assuming, *hoping* it's Alisha calling me back.

"Good afternoon, Miss Locket." Alexander's voice comes through the phone, and my heart stills. "I have an hour spare and was hoping you would join me for lunch."

I hesitate. Of course I want to. The giddy teenager in me is getting excited again that her crush is asking her out, but the side of me who has been battling with myself since this morning just doesn't know if she can take any more of him right now. *You only have him for two weeks.*

"Samantha?"

"Yeah, sorry I'm here. Yeah, umm, okay. Let's do it. I will be ready in ten minutes."

"I will be impatiently waiting." I don't mean it, but I immediately hang up without saying anything back. I don't want to change my mind, I don't think. Or perhaps going to lunch, somewhere public, is the perfect way to put an end to this before it has the chance to really start.

I get changed into another matching lace bra and panties set; this time they are red rather than black. I can't decide if I like the colour against my skin as much as the black. I make a mental note to perhaps not buy any more in the future and decide on a red long-sleeved mini dress that cinches in at the waist. I test it out in front of the mirror and realise pretty quickly I definitely won't be able to bend over, but the cute cut at the top that shapes perfectly around my breast makes it hard to convince myself to swap it out for something else. I make quick work of some light makeup and put my hair into a high pony. I pair the dress with a pair of black knee-high heeled boots. With one final glance in the mirror at the woman I don't recognise, I decide to call it. If I don't leave now, I will strip the disguise away, and if I do that, I'm not sure I will have the strength to do this face-to-face.

I pull back my shoulders and take a deep breath. *You have to do this.* I open the door and step out into the hall; I'm looking down at my phone to see if Alexander has messaged anything about where we are supposed to meet. Instead, there is finally a message from Alisha. I tap the message to open it, but a shift in front of me catches my eye. I assume it's Mr

Ridged who is usually out the front of what I am now assuming is Alexander's room. I look up to offer what I'm sure will be an unmet polite smile, but instead, my stomach is in immediate knots and my cheeks warm. Alexander is standing in front of me; he is wearing plain dress pants and a white button-up with the top button undone, just like on the plane. I go to say something, but my voice catches somewhere in the back of my throat. I can't do this. Just the sheer sight of him has me useless.

"Good afternoon, Miss Locket." His voice is like a warmth that envelops itself all around me.

"You look incredible." He looks me over in a way that makes my mouth immediately dry with nerves, but my cheeks warm.

"Good afternoon, Alexander." I finally manage to whisper.

"Ready for lunch?" He holds out his hand. I place my hand in his. There is a shift in the air around us. The noise of it all stops again, and it all feels empty, except for right here with *him*. He traces his thumb over mine, and something the equivalent of electricity travels up my arm. The surprise of it makes my heart skip. How is it possible to be this taken by another human? How is it possible for me to lie to his face and tell him I don't want to continue this with him anymore?

"I think so." I say weakly.

He leads us into the elevator, and I hold my breath as the doors close.

"How has your day been?" There is something behind his eyes, like he already knows something, and he is waiting to hear me say it. I won't give him the satisfaction of knowing I spend the whole morning after he left in a downward spiral because of him and me and us.

He says nothing but raises his eyebrow at me. It makes me fear my suspicions were right. His driver had messaged him when I got back to the room. The thought pisses me off, but by some miracle, I am able to keep my anger contained. There is no point kicking up a stink about it until I know for sure, and the only way I will know is if I ask Alexander about it.

The elevator doors open, and he leads me through the lobby and to the street outside. Parked directly out the front of the doors is a BMW. Alexander's driver moves from the front of the car to the back. He goes to open the door, but Alexander tells him he's got it.

"Sir." He replies and instead gets in the driver's seat.

Alexander lets go of my hand and opens the car door, "Samantha." He says as he stands, waiting expectantly for me to get in. I look from him to the driver, and a knot forms in my stomach, different from the one I feel when he is with me. I am vibrating with nerves.

"Did your driver tell you I had returned to the hotel?"

"Yes." His answer is careful. Like he is talking to some wild beast ready to pounce at him. He raises his eyebrow at me.

"Did he tell you I was unwell?"

"Not that you were, but yes, that you seemed like you might be."

"Alexander, that's fucked up. It's stalking. It's no one's business when I come and go from anywhere, not his or yours."

He lets go of the door and comes towards me. I instinctively step back, and for just a blink, that same lost man from this morning is back, but he quickly recovers.

"I apologise; I can see why that would have been intrusive. I promise you I didn't ask to know when you returned because of ill intent. It was just to make sure you were safe."

"Alexander, that's ridiculous, of course I was safe."

He looks around at the busy street around us and steps closer; this time, I let him. His voice is low in the way that makes my cheeks blush.

"Samantha, please, get in the car. You're making a scene. We can continue this conversation in privacy."

All I can offer him in response to his boldness is a scoff.

"Samantha, please, unless you want to find yourself in the tabloids by five tonight, I suggest you either get in the car or we can cancel lunch and go our separate ways." He runs a frustrated hand through his hair again.

He is giving me an out, I can turn around right now, go back to my room and begin pretending the last two days didn't happen. I can restart my holiday and forget the part that includes meeting any damn men. I could, but I don't. Instead, I walk past him and slide into the back of the car. He closes my door, but not before I catch him mutter a relieved "Thank God." Under his breath.

He gets in the other side of the car, and I watch as his driver looks at Alexander through the rear-view mirror and gives each other a small nod before the driver pulls out into the flow of traffic. A smooth instrumental song that I don't recognise fills the car, it's just barely enough to hear it, but loud enough in the quiet between us.

"I know you are conflicted about us." Alexander's voice is low.

"Alexander, whatever this is, it's... "I try to find the words to perfectly sum up the last few days. Hot, intense, exciting, new, terrifying. "It's fast. I'm only here for two weeks. We were all over each other after barely twelve hours of meeting. Whatever this is, it's never going to last beyond the time I'm here, so what's the point in letting it go beyond what we already have?" There, I did it, I got it out. I relax my shoulders and slump back in the seat.

The car is silent, and I watch as Alexander wordlessly reaches his hand out across the empty middle seat between us. I once again place my hand in his, and it happens again. There is no longer music lulling in the background, no honking horns outside or road noise. A warm buzz feeling runs up my arms and shivers down the length of my spine, and my stomach knots.

"That's the point." He is breathless and looks just as confused and perhaps curious. As me.

"Alexander, I don't know." I can't bear to look at him, so I watch the city fly past through what I'm sure are barely legal tinted windows.

"Samantha, please, I know you're affected by whatever this is, too." His eyes darken, and his lips part ever so slightly. "I don't have it in me to stay away from you, Samantha."

In a matter of seconds, I have unbuckled my seatbelt, and I am sitting on him with my legs either side of his. I tangle my hands in his hair and kiss him. It's desperate and full of need. He traces my bottom lip with his tongue, and I open wider to let him in. His hands trace down my back and cup my arse. He lifts me up a little, shifting him over his hardening erection. My hips rock back and forth over him, and he sucks in a breath through clenched teeth. I shift again and hit just the right spot. Pleasure shoots through me as he kisses me again, dissolving my moan into him. He pulls back out of the kiss and rests his finger under my chin.

"You need to get back in your seat."

I pout dramatically. "What if I don't want to?" I taunt and rock my hips over him again.

His breath hitches, and his eyes darken "Damn it, Samantha, I will fuck you right here if you keep this up. I don't give a shit if Logan sees, do you?" He growls.

Holy fuck the whole situation is hot. I've never had sex in a car before, or in front of someone else. But right now, I want nothing more than to do this, with Alexander, in the back of his car. I glance behind me at Logan, and I consider the repercussions of doing this. I'm not sure I would ever be able to look Mr stalker assistant in the face again. . . I shift again, half getting off Alexander's lap.

"Good girl." He whispers right at my ear and bites the lobe.

Fuck.

"I don't care." I whisper back and reposition myself back on him.

"What are you doing to me?" He is breathy and his eyes are full of desire.

"Giving you what you want."

The music is louder and filling the car. Alexander looks up briefly and nods, I assume to Logan as an acknowledgement of him turning the music up.

He plants light kisses along my jawline, trailing down along my throat. My head rolls back, exposing more of my skin to him. He continues down, planting feather-light kisses on the tops of my breasts. He pulls the top of my dress and bra down together, and the underwire of my bra makes my breasts sit high and ready. My nipples harden under his gaze. Every inch of my skin craves his touch, and I rock my hips again, needing to feel some sort of friction. He places both hands on my hips and holds me in place.

"Stay still for me, baby."

"Alexander please." I plead.

"Not yet." he holds me in place but continues kissing my breasts, working his way slowly over them and then down until he reaches the nipple of my left breast. He flicks his tongue over it, then moves on to the other and does the same thing. He lingers on the right a little longer, alternating between licking and biting.

"I'm going to let go of your hips. Stay still."

I reply with some version of the word "okay."

He reaches down into his front pocket, making me need to shift to my utter frustration. He pulls his wallet out, and I raise my eyebrow at him curiously.

He makes a point of showing me the condom packet he is pulling out.

This is actually about to happen.

He puts the foil packet to the side of us on the seat and lets me position myself back on his lap properly. His rock-hard erection feels like he is about to burst through the material of his pants at any moment. I move in just the right way to send another shock of pleasure through myself again, and I moan.

"Move back." He growls.

I do as I'm told, and he picks up the foil packet. He goes back to torturing my left nipple. I can't wait any longer. If he makes me, I'm going to come already, and I don't want to without him.

I reach down and undo his belt. I wait for him to protest, but instead, as I undo his button and zip, he lifts so I can shift his pants down. I finally free him from his pants and immediately wrap my hand around his impressive length. I squeeze and move my hand up and down, watching his mouth go slack, and his eyes roll back in response.

"Put it on." He hands me the foil packet. We don't break eye contact as I tear the packet with my teeth, toss the packet to the side and roll the condom down his cock.

"Tell me what you want, Samantha."

"You." I breathe.

Move your underwear to the side. I get up higher on my knees, making my breasts line up perfectly with his face and do as he says. There is an appreciative hum in his chest, and it makes my stomach clench.

"We don't have long until we get there, so I'm going to fuck you now, Samantha. I'm going to make you come quick. Are you ready?"

"Yes." Is all I can manage.

"Good girl." He repeats, and I fear I'm going to come before we've even started.

He grabs my hips again and positions himself at my opening. He pushes his waist up, and inch by inch, I feel myself stretch and fill around him. He pauses once he is completely in, and I adjust to the feeling of fullness, but the pause is quickly cut short.

"Lean your waist forward a little."

I do as I'm told, and it makes it so we are perfectly positioned for my clit to rub against him. I moan appreciatively, and he picks up pace, thrusting over and over. I match him thrust for thrust.

"Fuck." I call out and bury my head in his neck. But move immediately back into place when I realise I have shifted from the sweet spot.

Without losing pace, he once again flicks his tongue over my nipple.

Every sensation feels heightened, my body tenses around him, and I become hyperaware of every feeling. His fullness, his tongue, the delicious sensation radiating from my clit to everywhere else throughout my body. The tension becomes tighter. It's never felt like this before with anyone else.

"Come for me, Samantha." The sound of my name coming from him in such a desperate, lust-filled way is enough to tip me over the edge.

"Alexander." I call out a garbled version of his name, and he moves his hands from my hips to my arse. He grabs tightly and continues for three more thrusts before he meets me in finishing.

"Fuck." He stills in me, and I give him a minute to make sure he is completely done before I clamber off his lap.

He makes quick work of removing the condom, tying it off and discarding it in a little bin that is attached to the bottom of the door. I give him a moment of privacy to fix himself up and do my best to re-wrangle my hair into an as neat as possible ponytail.

Logan turns the music back down, and just as I knew I would, I let the realisation of what we have just done in front of him hit me. I can't seem to find it in me to look up at Alexander, no matter how much I want to.

"Sir?" Logan asks.

"Go ahead," Alexander responds with a smile.

Logan picks up a box from the passenger seat that I hadn't noticed. I don't know how I hadn't, it's too big to fit on the seat.

A sheepish look crosses Alexander's face as he hands it to me.

"Alexander, no, I don't need gifts."

He shakes his head. "Please just take it."

Reluctantly, I take the box. It's exquisite, dark navy blue with a lighter blue ribbon tied into a perfect bow. I untie the delicate ribbon carefully and remove the lid. I gasp at the bunch of long-stemmed roses inside the box.

"Alexander, they're beautiful."

"Here." he says and reaches over to the box of roses and pulls out a little red jewellery box that matches the colour of the petals perfectly, sitting in the bottom of the box.

He holds it so it's facing me and opens it. Inside sits a beautiful silver heart-shaped locket with the letter A engraved on it. A tiny red rose sits on the upper right of the heart, matching the ones in the box. My mind is reeling with a confusing mix of overwhelm and excitement.

"This is too much; how did you get this organised so quickly? How did you even know I would join you for lunch?"

"I didn't know if you would, especially out the front of the hotel, but I hoped." A hint of a shy smile crosses his face, and it's his turn for his cheeks to pink.

He places the little box, still open, back with the flowers. "There's no pressure for you to have to associate the A with my name, although I have to admit that was the intention. There truly is nothing more fitting a gift for you, Miss Locket."

He reaches his hand out again. I once again unbuckle my seatbelt, carefully put the lid back on and put it back on the front passenger seat. I climb across the seat and curl myself up on his lap, resting my head on his chest. "Thank you, Alexander."

Ten

"Alexander, this is incredible." He pulls me toward the front of the boat, but he is walking far too quickly, leaving me no chance to even come to terms with the fact that I am standing on a yacht. We reach the bow, where there is a waiting table that looks big enough to seat six, but there are only two chairs. The chairs closely match the sandy wood floors of the boat, and the table is covered by a crisp white cloth, matching the rest of the boat and already laid out with wine glasses, pates, hand towels and a crystal vase with blue tulips. *I didn't even know they came in blue.*

"Sit." Alexander commands while pulling out one of the chairs.

He joins me at the table. A clean-cut, young-looking man dressed in a white button-up and white trousers comes over to the table holding a bottle of wine. He says nothing as he pours the white wine into each of our glasses. A light breeze crosses the boat, carrying with it the smell of the ocean. The warm October sun is divine on my skin, but the way it feels is nothing compared to the way the gold in Alexander's eyes gleams under its glow.

"Hungry?"

I trace my index finger over my lips, images flash behind my eyes of his lips on mine in the car. My breath catches.

"Starving."

He leans forward a little and takes a drink from his wine.

"You're insatiable, Miss Locket; we are going to have to work on your greedy appetite." Never before have I had someone make me feel so completely exposed, flushed and wanting with mere words. He puts his drink down, leans back in his chair and lets his legs sprawl out in front of him. My mouth dries as he removes his tie and undoes his top two shirt buttons. He places the tie on the table in front of him, and my eyes flicker from it and back to him. I subconsciously wrap my fingers around my wrist.

"You could fix it, or you could give me what I want.

"And what exactly is it you want, Samantha?"

"I want you to finish what you started with that tie." He sits back up and leans in again.

"There is something I have to discuss with you. If you decide you still want to continue seeing me, then I will happily oblige. Otherwise, if you decide otherwise, Logan is on standby to take you home."

It's my turn to take a drink. My mind buzzes with every possible thing he could want to discuss.

He wants to just hook up? He didn't get all of his money legally? He is into something weird?

"Breathe, Samantha." I do as I'm told and take another drink from it's a blend of citrus and oak and it's divine.

"I will no longer be staying at the hotel; I was only staying there because I was having some renovations done in my home that are now complete."

"Oh?" I drop my shoulders with relief. "Do you not live on the coast? I just assumed."

"I live in South Brisbane. But that's not what I need to discuss with you." He straightens his back and takes yet another drink. "Samantha, there is a reason we are on my boat right now for lunch and not at some restaurant. I have a stalker. It's an ex of mine. It ended badly when she became obsessive. I put an end to it when she became abusive, but she hasn't taken it so well." His wall is down again, exposing his vulnerability.

Holy shit, this isn't even remotely what I expected. I think about the phone calls I have overheard him on and realise how blind I've been.

"Is she dangerous?"

"I'm afraid she could be. I wouldn't have thought so when we first got together, but she showed her true self after six months, and now, honestly, I don't know."

I finish my wine. *You could have ended this before getting in the car.* The stupid, usually always right voice in my head screams at me.

"Samantha, I don't know if I'm ready to do this. I only left her two months ago, and honestly, she had me in a pretty fucked state. I know I shouldn't be sitting here right now sharing yet another meal with you, I should never have allowed what we did in the car."

I didn't want this either. I left the hotel with every intention of putting a stop to all of this, and yet every word he speaks makes the burning lump in my throat get worse, and tears begin to well.

"This is why you apologised earlier." I whisper, speaking my thoughts out loud.

"Yes."

"I completely understand if you want to leave. Like I said. Logan is waiting, just say the word."

"I don't want to go anywhere." I wait for the screaming voice in my head to call me an idiot or to tell me to take it back, but it never comes, and truthfully, I know it's because, for some stupid reason, I meant it.

***

"Stand here. Don't move." Alexander crosses the bedroom and opens one of the high gloss walnut coloured cupboard doors. He presses a few buttons on his phone, and a beautiful instrumental piece fills the room from the speakers behind the cupboard doors. I watch every move as he makes his way around the room, closing the blackout blinds on all four windows on the left side of the room, followed by the ones on the right. He stops at a drawer and opens it. He pulls something silver out and immediately puts it in his pocket. My stomach churns, threatening to bring up the chicken alfredo and wine. I'm not sure if it's from the light movement on the water or if it's the building nerves.

He picks his tie back up from the bed. "Come stand by this bedpost."

He points to one of the mahogany posts on the king-sized four-poster bed that sits in the middle of the room. The sandy coloured bedding, matching pillows, and cushions look completely untouched.

"I thought you only had an hour." My voice is small, and I cuss myself out for my returning vulnerability showing.

He traces his fingers up my arm, sending warm shivers all over.

"I made other arrangements. Turn."

I turn so I'm facing the bed, my heart hammers so hard I'm scared it's going to force its way straight through my chest. He runs his fingers along both arms, then across my shoulder blades. He stops at the top of my zip, and excruciatingly slowly, he pulls it down. He gets to the bottom of the zip and moves to my shoulders. He slides the dress down from my shoulders, making it fall to my feet. My breath hitches.

"Breathe, Samantha." His lips are at my ear, and his hands are on my hips. He spins me around, so I am facing him again.

"Put your arms up." I raise my eyebrow at him, but oblige.

He pulls the silver thing from his pocket. *Oh.* He attaches one side of the handcuffs to the bedpost. He picks up his tie from the bed.

"Tell me what you want baby." He kisses me before I get a chance to answer. It's swift and leaves me wanting.

"You." I breathe.

He binds the tie around my wrists, the sound of the unused half of the handcuff clicks, then he ties off the tie onto it. He pulls down a little on the handcuffs.

My stomach clenches, and I'm panting more than breathing. Every inch of me is begging for him to touch me.

He pulls a set of tiny keys from his pocket. "At any point if you need to stop, I will undo you."

All I can manage is a nod in response. I'm afraid that if I try to speak, nothing is going to come out.

"This is important, Samantha. I mean it, all you have to do is say stop, and we are done. You need to answer me properly; tell me you understand."

"I understand." I breathe.

He takes a step back, and his eyes travel down the entirety of my body. "You are a siren, Samantha Locket." His voice is gravel, and the sound of him makes heat travel all over.

He steps back toward me and kisses me again, to my absolute disappointment, it's another quick one. "Alexander." I plead. He shakes his head in response and instead lines my jaw with feather-light kisses. He trails down to my breast and kisses the top of the left one. I writhed against my restraint, and he stops kissing me.

He glides his hand down my body, and I think he is going to stop at the top of my underwear, but he just hovers there for a second. He reaches into my underwear and immediately circles my clit with his finger. I suck in a sharp breath as pleasure courses through me.

All too quickly, he moves on to my opening. He traces around my entrance twice before thrusting his finger inside me, at a lazy pace, he removes it and thrusts it back in.

"So easily ready for me, Miss Locket."

I can't seem to form words. All I can focus on is his words, his hands, his smell. *Him.*

He removes his finger and circles my clit again. he lingers with a slow pace and leans in to kiss me again. he lingers this time, but it's not like every other time. He is slow and delicate. He bites my bottom lip, and I moan into him.

He stops again and removes his hand from my underwear. He hooks his thumbs in at my hips and slides them down, then drops to his knees. Faster than I have time to register, he is looking up at me, then his mouth is on me. His tongue circles my clit expertly, and waves of pleasure course through me. heat builds up in my entire body, and I moan again and pull against the handcuffs. I push my hips forward, pushing myself closer to him.

"Alexander, please." I beg, but I don't even know what it is I'm begging for. I want him to tip me over the edge, but I don't want it to end. I want him to fuck me, but I don't want him to stop what he is doing.

He stops circling my clit and instead licks from my entrance back to my clit then gets to his feet.

"You're divine baby."

He goes back to the same drawer before and comes back with a foil packet.

"Are you ready?" his voice is low and hot.

"Yes."

He undoes his shirt and removes it, then follows with his pants and briefs. I suck in a breath at the sight of him.

I realise he is close enough for me reach and I take advantage of the opportunity. I grip his cock in my hand and squeeze. Stroking him from back to tip. He sucks in a breath through clenched teeth and the sight of him so taken by such a simple act being done by me is the most powerful thing I've ever felt. I continue on, squeezing and stroking him, but not for as long as I would like. He holds his hand over mine and gently removes it.

He undoes the packet and rolls the condom onto himself. He grips my hips again and turns me so I'm facing the bed. I feel the warmth of his body as he positions himself behind me. He lightly separates my feet by pushing them apart with his foot. He reaches around and locates my clit, picking back up where he left off earlier, but it only lasts seconds before his fingers once again find my opening. He inserts and removes his finger only once, but it's enough for my stomach muscles to clench.

He brings his hand up to my face.

"Open." He growls in my ear, and as soon as I do, his fingers are in my mouth. I suck the slightly salty wetness off his fingers.

"Good little siren."

I roll my head back so it's resting on his shoulder and moan.

"Don't hold your breath." His shoulder is gone, and I hold my head back up.

He positions his cock at my opening and, without warning, thrusts himself into me. I cry out in a garbled mix of pleasure and shock. He keeps himself inside me while putting his hands on my hips. He digs his nails in until they are just on the verge of hurting. Once he is satisfied with his positioning, he pulls almost all the way back out, then immediately thrusts back in. He keeps a fast rhythmic pace. Over and over, he thrusts in and out of me. I hold the chain on the handcuff and pull against them; I push back against him, willing for more. Pressure builds, and my body begins to still and tense around him.

"That's it, baby, come for me." he continues, thrusting, and the building is becoming unbearable.

"Alexander." I beg.

"I know baby." He says, and he reaches around to my clit, somehow managing to keep his pace. His fingers find my clit, and it takes only seconds for me to find my release around him.

"Alexander." I cry out as I tense around him.

"Good job. Little. Siren." He says between each thrust as he, too, finds his release.

Eleven

It doesn't seem possible, but the shower on the boat seems somehow better than the one in the hotel room. I rub my wrist where the tie and handcuffs have been. Red marks that are already starting to fade are all the confirmation I need that this is all really happening. I'm really on a boat owned by a hot *something -an -aire*. I really gave myself to him unashamedly in the back of his car, then again just now in the master suite… of his boat. The last few days have been a whirlwind. Just days ago, I was at work being harassed by Yates and now… stars form around my eyes, my vision blurs, and my head spins. As fast as I can, I turn the shower off, wrap the towel around myself and go to the sink.

I brace myself against the granite and take a few steadying breaths. My phone buzzes, making a welcome distraction I hope to use to distract from the anxiety growing in my chest.

Alisha: "Hey girl, sorry I didn't pick
Up. My interview was moved
To today… You're looking at
the new regional manager!
I start as soon as I come
back from my time off.
I'm sorting out a flight now
hoping to fly out tomorrow.

I re-read Alisha's message. The anxiety dulls. I think that's what I have needed this whole time. I need my best friend to tell everything to. She's never going to believe any of it unless she meets him in person for herself.

I get dressed, feeling a little uncomfortable with the idea of having to put the same clothes back on after showering. I tie my hair back up into a ponytail and call it job done.

When I walk out of the bathroom and into the adjoining master suite, Alexander is nowhere to be seen, but all of the blinds have been opened back up, and any sign that I was tied to the bed has been cleaned away. I continue through to the huge living area, it's all-white walls, brass hardware and huge windows. There is a cream-coloured half-moon-shaped sofa. To the right of the room, Alexander is sitting at a desk that looks big enough to sit six people. He is typing something on his laptop and has his phone to his ear, seemingly listening to someone on the other end.

"I have just sent through the email you requested. I have the Japan meeting on the twelfth of next month that I also need you to book accommo-dation for." I watch as he finishes up something on the laptop and leans back in his seat. He runs his hand through his hair and frowns.

"Well, let's hope the meeting goes well so we can guarantee we are back by the fourteenth." he rubs the bridge of his nose and sighs. "No, it's fine. I will handle it. Thank you, Laura. No, that's every-thing for now."

"Everything okay?" I cross the room to him and sit in one of the two chairs on the opposite side of the desk.

"Everything is perfect." He manages a small smile, but it doesn't touch his eyes.

"If you have work you need to do, I can leave if you want me to." I hope that he can't see through me. I, of course, will leave if he does need to work, but I won't be happy about it. I'm also more than happy, stalling having to see Logan again any time soon.

"The last thing I want is for you to go anywhere. I do, however, need to get some work done, and I'm sure you would much rather explore the boat than watch me work."

My teeth bite into my bottom lip. "I don't know, I'm sure there are worse things I can sit and watch."

Alexander shakes his head and chuckles.

"Fine, I relent. I am afraid I won't be able to get my work done while you are here. Every time I look at you, I have to fight everything in myself to not touch you. Even now, I want nothing more than to bend you over this desk and take you."

I lean in closer and rest my elbow on the desk. I rest my chin on my hand and trace my index finger over my bottom lip. "In that case, maybe I will stay right here."

He sits up in his seat, the air around us becomes electric. His eyes darken with need. "I think maybe you should."

The silence between us is interrupted by his phone ringing.

Alexander clears his throat. "I'm sorry. I have to take this." He gives an apologetic smile.

I wave him off and leave the living area through the huge doors that lead back out to the bow. I make my way along the side of the boat and look out at the vast sea surrounding us. There is only a handful of small clouds in the sky, and the sun's light reflection on the ocean ripples is like a shimmering night sky.

"Can I get you anything to drink, ma'am?" The voice startles me. I turn to see that it is the same man who bought us our lunch. I nearly say no thank you, but I'm suddenly aware that my throat is drying. I figure it's the sea air causing it.

"Yes, please, whatever you have available is fine."

"Ma'am, we have a completely stocked kitchen and wine fridge. If you have anything particular you would like, I am sure I can put it together for you."

I knew the boat was big, but I didn't realise it was kitchen with staff working in it big.

"The same wine we had with lunch will be fine, thank you." He hurries off, and I take a seat at the table we ate lunch at and pull my phone out. There is a generic notification from the job-hunting app, so I open it and have a quick look to see if any new listings have gone up that I can apply for.

There is an ad for an insurance call centre position in Brisbane. I open the ad to read what is needed to apply, then shake my head at myself. I can't *actually* be considering this. My wine arrives, and as I continue to scroll through jobs, I sip continuously at my wine. Sooner than expected, the glass is empty, and I feel flushed. I chastise myself for being so heavy-handed with yet another drink and continue looking through the ads. The same job bobs up again, but this time I hit the apply button, I upload my resume, and I answer the handful of 'about me' questions. I rationalise what I've done once I hit the final apply button by reassuring myself that it's completely unlikely that I will get the job anyway.

Alexander comes out of the same large doors I did earlier. His hair is dishevelled, and even from a few good feet away, I can see on his face that something is wrong.

Rather than sitting with me, he stands to the side of me.

"Alexander, what is it?"

He sighs, a long-winded sigh, and I can see that he is struggling to say what he needs.

"I mean it, if you need me to leave, I'm happy to. Just as soon as we get back to shore."

He shakes his head. "We are on our way back to shore now. Something has happened, and I need to ask you something. I understand if you want to say no, but I really need you to consider that I'm asking you to do this for a good reason."

He grabs my hands and pulls me up to him. He rests his hand on my hip.

"Come stay in Brisbane with me tonight."

My mouth immediately dries.

I wrap my arms around his lower waist and look up at him.

"Alexander, I don't think that's a good idea. We are already moving impossibly fast. I've barely known you for twenty-four hours and already we have done it twice, nearly three times. This isn't me.

I don't behave like this ever, and honestly, I think I want to go back to my room, read on the balcony and order room service for my dinner."

His whole body stiffens.

"I can't make you, but I will insist."

I step back, putting some space between us. "I'm sorry, Alexander. I'm not comfortable with it."

He pinches the bridge of his nose and sighs. "Someone has been accessing my emails."

"Your ex?"

"I don't know, I have people finding that out as we speak, but I suspect."

Holy shit.

"Either way, I need to return to the office in Brisbane now to do some damage control. It's not a good look when a bank that prides itself on the tightest security on the market has a CEO who is experiencing a security breach on his personal accounts. If you want to go back to the hotel, then I will respect your wishes and take you back."

Twelve

The car ride back to the hotel is silent. Alexander doesn't let go of my hand once. Even through the countless phone calls to so many different people who are updating him on the search for the stalker and repairing any damage they can find that has been done. I give him an occasional reassuring squeeze ever so often, and every time, without fail, he does his best to give me a reassuring smile.

The hotel comes into view, and Alexander undoes both his and my seatbelt. He reaches around my waist and scoops me into his lap. I rest my head on his chest and breathe him in. he smells of soap and a hint of sandalwood. He tucks a loose thread of hair behind my ear. "Last chance. Are you sure you won't reconsider and come spend the night with me?" He traces his fingers up my thigh and plants a soft kiss on the top of my head.

Warmth travels from my thighs to every inch of my body. The thought is tempting. The curious side of me would love a look into who Alexander is when he is in his home. I imagine him sitting on a sofa, reading or cooking dinner for himself in some obnoxiously huge kitchen. The thought makes me smile, but I need to stand my ground. I need space to think, to come to terms with the last few days and to just be alone again, where I'm comfortable. Well, as comfortable as I can be away from my falling-apart farmhouse. I hadn't realised I was growing homesick this quickly. I decide that when I get back to the hotel, I need to call mum and ask her to swing by and check on the house for me.

"I'm sure." I whisper, hoping I sound convincing.

Logan brings the car to a stop, and Alexander tightens his arms around me. "Make sure you call me if you need anything."

"I will."

I climb off his lap, and to my surprise, he gets out of the car. He makes his way around and opens my door.

As soon as I am out of the car, he tilts my chin, forcing me to look at him.

"I mean it, if you need anything at all, you call me. I will be right back here.

I don't get the chance to tell him not to worry about me, to do whatever he needs to fix the problems caused by his ex. His mouth is on mine, devouring every unspoken word. It's slow, deep and full of need.

When he pulls away, he can't seem to hide the concern in his eyes.

"Alexander, I will be fine." I put my hand against the side of his face, and he covers my hand with his. He lets his face lean into my hand. He closes his eyes and sighs.

"Think of me, baby." He gives me a swift kiss and all to soon, he is getting back in the car.

***

The room is quiet and empty, and the initial excitement I had when I first arrived seems long gone. The knowledge that Alexander is no longer right next door, or in my room, is creating a pit in my stomach. I put the huge box containing the roses on the dining table. That's a whole other issue for me to unpack later. I pace around the room contemplating what I can busy myself with, then settle on making a coffee and reading on the balcony. I get set up and scroll through the eBook store until I find a book about a billionaire who falls in love with a *normal* girl. I settle in with my coffee and book and let myself completely lose myself in the cliché that is somehow impossibly turning into my real life.

I take the final sip of my now-cold coffee. My phone rings as I put my mug down, and I can't help my smile when I see Alisha's name on my screen.

"I'm flying in late tomorrow night." She practically shouts before I can even say hello.

"Thank God. I already have so much to tell you."

"Listen, I can't wait to hear all about it, but I can't stay on the phone long. I just wanted to tell you instead of texting you. Also, tomorrow night I need you to meet me at a club called Lola's. it's not far from the hotel. I will send you the address. They are doing a Halloween theme, and I promised some other friends I would join them when I was planning this holiday. I won't have much time between landing and the time we arranged to meet."

"Alisha, what the fuck?" I'm usually fantastic at withholding my anger with her, but every so often, I lose the battle. "You can't just spring this on me. Don't you think you should have told me you planned on us meeting up with other people at a fucking club before the day before? You know I can't stand shit like this, and even if I do agree to go, what the fuck am I supposed to wear?" It's my turn to run my hands through my hair in exasperation.

"Oh, don't be like that. This is exactly *why* I didn't tell you. This holiday is meant to include you getting out of your comfort zone."

I snort. If only she knew just how out of my comfort zone I have already been.

"Right, I need to go. Just put on something cute and get creative with your makeup; it will be enough. I will see you tomorrow night."

I don't have it in me to continue an argument I know I'm going to lose.

"Goodbye, Alisha." She hangs up, and I fall back in my chair.

I attempt to go back to my book, but I can't focus. I'm beyond frustrated at Alisha and her once again dictating my decisions. I contemplate calling Alexander, but it seems ridiculous. Nothing is wrong besides being mad at my best friend, and calling him about that seems incredibly childish, especially with what he is dealing with.

Instead, I decide to wave my mental white flag and accept Alisha's plans. That was the whole point of me being part of this holiday. There is no point arguing with her, at the bare minimum, I can show up for an hour tops so I can be a decent friend and do something she wants to do, then call it a night.

I do a quick web search for the closest clothing boutiques in the hopes I can find a new dress for tomorrow night. There is one only a block away, so I decide tomorrow morning I will start there. For now, the rest of my night will consist of more job hunting, ordering room service up to my room for dinner, watching trashy TV, and doing everything I can to keep Alexander as far out of my mind as possible. It's more difficult than I had accomplished and throughout the night, I do find myself letting my mind drift to him. I wonder about what he is doing. I wonder if he has worked out the issues with his stalker. I worry that he hasn't, and he is more stressed out than earlier tonight.

As I lay in bed, covered by fresh crisp linens and let my eyelids grow heavy as the dull sound of some game show plays on the TV, I allow myself to respond to the message Alexander had sent earlier in the night, saying he is having a hard time in the meeting, he keeps having thoughts of handcuffs and the sea.

His message makes me giggle, and I shake my head.

Me: Mr Truette, I never
Took you as an easily
distracted man. Perhaps
We should put an end
To our distracting activities
To ensure you don't lose your position
At work.

I manage to stay awake just long enough to receive a response from him.

Alexander: Miss Locket, Interestingly
I was never an easily distracted

Man, until I met you.
Get some sleep, it's late, and
You just made a ridiculous
Suggestion, you're clearly
Not thinking clearly.

I roll onto my stomach and prop myself up on my elbows. How incredibly rude of him to suggest that I'm not serious. I'm not, mostly, there is still a corner in my mind flashing red alarm lights and blasting a siren telling me to get the hell out. This is going too fast, this is way out of my comfort zone, and he is way out of my league. I can feel another mental spiral coming on, and I'm too damn tired to have to deal with it right now.

Good night, Alexander.

I hit send, toss my phone somewhere beside me on the bed and flop down dramatically off my elbows and onto the too soft pillow. Panic threatens to once again bubble up, but I let my heavy eyelids win the battle and give in to sleep instead. Letting myself drift off to the feel of hands gliding up my thighs and his tongue *there*.

Thirteen

I trace my fingers over a charcoal mini skirt. I decide it will be perfect for the club tonight and pair it with a dark red off-the-shoulder long-sleeved top. I plan to wear it with my knee-high boots. All the frustration I was feeling last night has been swapped with excitement to finally see her again and start doing this holiday like we were supposed to, together. I do tend to let myself forget that me doing something

Alisha wants is just as much of a rare occasion as her doing what I want. Friendship is all about compromise and meeting each other halfway, so that is exactly what I plan to do as much as I can, especially considering the insane amount she spent on us being on this holiday. Making sure we spend this holiday doing things she wants to do is the right thing. While also somehow *hopefully* spending time with Alexander. Assuming he even has time with everything going on. I haven't heard from him yet, and it's already midday. I have considered messaging him multiple times since I woke up, but have decided against it every time. The solitude has been nice. Exploring by myself, eating breakfast, and shopping all by myself has been exactly what I needed.

I take the long way back to the hotel once I have finished clothes shopping. The midday sun is beautiful on my skin, but is making me regret the decision to go comfortable today in a cream-coloured long-sleeved top. The blue boyfriend shorts are, of course, fine.

I notice a little café with a sign saying air conditioner within, and that's all the convincing I need.

I order a Caesar salad, an ice water and an over-ice coffee with hazelnut syrup and whipped cream in a to-go cup. Once I'm done eating, I take my coffee and sip at it on the walk back to the hotel.

The elevator door opens to my floor, and I fumble with my bags, phone, key card and coffee.

I drop my phone just as I step out of the elevator. Before I get the chance to pick it up, someone is picking it up.

"Logan?" I gasp as he hands me my phone.

"He isn't here, Miss." He says as my eyes dart around the hallway. His words make my stomach drop. If Alexander isn't here, why is Logan? Has something happened to him, and Logan is here to tell me?

"Then why are you here?" I ask the question, but I'm afraid I'm not going to want to hear the answer.

He pulls his shoulders back and clears his throat. "My job, Miss."

"Your job as his driver is to stand in a hallway in a hotel room in a completely different city than your employer?" he raises his eyebrow and tilts his head forward a little. *Oh no.* "You're here for me, aren't you?"

"Yes, Miss." He nods and keeps his tone level. But the reddening of his cheeks tells me he is just as uncomfortable with this as I am.

"Logan, this really is over the top. I'm on the nineteenth floor of a hotel that you can't get to without the key card. I'm perfectly safe."

"I'm afraid he insisted I be here, Miss and frankly, so do I."

This is insane. He has a crazy ex-girlfriend. I get that. But having his driver, who is very obviously a fucking henchman hiding under the guise of a driver waiting for me to arrive back to my room and keeping tabs on me, again, is frankly too fucking far. I say nothing further to him. I go into my room and call Alexander.

He picks up on the third ring.

"I know you aren't happy about Logan being there. Please understand that I just need to know you are safe while I can't be with you. This isn't something I would normally do, especially without your permission, but because you didn't want to come home with me and I can't be there with you, I need Logan there."

It sounds as if he has rehearsed exactly what it was, he was going to say to me. He does genuinely seem embarrassed, but that doesn't change the fact that knowing I can't do anything without feeling Like Logan is watching me is going to drive me nuts. Never mind me having no idea how the hell I'm supposed to explain something like that to Alisha when she gets here tonight. *Sorry, Alisha, we can still enjoy our holiday, but anytime we go anywhere, there is going to be a guy watching us.* yeah, that's going to go over well.

"Alexander, I understand that you have things going on and want to make sure I'm safe, but this is completely unnecessary. My friend is flying in tonight, so I won't be alone, so you don't have to worry, and I have no plans to leave my room be-tween now and later tonight when I meet up with her. I don't need Logan here."

There is silence on the other side of the phone. It's finally broken when he sighs.

"This isn't an argument I'm going to win, is it?" he asks quietly.

"Afraid not."

"Alright, look, I have to go. I will send Logan out of the hotel."

"Why do I feel like there is a catch?" I can't help the smile as I shake my head at him and pinch the bridge of my nose.

"It would appear you already know me so well, Miss Locket."

"Somehow I doubt that."

The voice of a woman comes through the phone from somewhere in the distance telling Alexander his eleven am meeting is waiting for him.

"Are you sure you won't reconsider? I can have Logan bring you to my house. Knowing you would be there, waiting for me when I finish work tonight might just be exactly what I need to make it through the full day of meetings and presentations I have today."

I hate that he sounds so hopeful, knowing that I can't say yes.

"I have plans tonight, I can't. I'm sorry." Surprisingly, I think I genuinely am sorry. Hearing him say he wants me waiting for him to come home makes my heart hammer. This feeling is different; it isn't the lust-filled need we've had up until this point. This is a completely different kind of need, one that a bigger part of me than I'm willing to admit to wants to fulfil.

"Goodbye, Alexander."

"Goodbye, my little siren."

Damn him and the things this man does to me with just words.

Immediately, there is a new message on my phone.

Alexander: Thinking of you, the sea and handcuffs.

Alexander: Looking forward
 to seeing you again little siren.
 In the meantime, I am
Going to send you Logan's
number. If something
 seems wrong in any way.
 Call him.

There is no point in adding to the stress he is already dealing with. Being the reason for just one more thing to be on his plate is the last thing I want to do, so as much as I would love to argue my point and tell him I don't need Logan's number, and I definitely will not be contacting him, I instead respond with just a thank you.

Fourteen

I take far longer than I should have in the shower. My fingers and toes are wrinkled and stinging. I'm going to need a good half hour to get ready after I get out, and I'm already running forty-five minutes late. I'm excited to see Alisha, but the homebody in me wants to stay here and wait it out for her to finish her night. The temptation to call her and tell her exactly that is almost too strong to fight against. *Almost.*

I get out and do my best to make quick work of getting dry and dressed. I don't bother with cute matching underwear this time. Just black cotton and a basic black bra. I huff at the realisation that I have purchased an off-the-shoulder top for tonight, but don't have a strapless bra. I tuck the straps of my bra into the sides of itself. It feels ridiculous, but once the top is on, I call it good enough.

I finish my make-up with a cat eye liner and red lip, it's far more dramatic than my normal look. Just like the rest of this holiday has been so far. I brush my hair and decide to just leave it out. Once I'm satisfied, I leave the bathroom and go in search of my boots. I pass the dining table on the way and spot the box of flowers and locket from Alexander. I don't really have the time, but I need to do something I should have done as soon as I arrived back at the hotel. I call down to the lobby and ask if they have any vases and scissors. The incredibly sweet-sounding woman on the phone informs me that they do, and she will send someone up with them right away.

I open the box of flowers. I have only ever been given flowers by my mother. They are exquisite. I pick up one of the roses and trace my fingers over one of the deep crimson petals. It's soft against my skin and so incredibly delicate. The thought of anything about Alexander being delicate makes me chuckle to myself. The little box sitting in the bottom corner catches my attention. I put the rose back down and pick up the box holding the locket. It truly is a beautiful gift, insane, especially after only a day, but beautiful nonetheless. I take it out of box and put it on. A strange feeling of heaviness seems to accompany it. Instinctively, I know this feeling is the logical side of me screaming *You know this is all too much too quickly. Wearing this damn necklace is basically saying you're okay with that.* The problem is, I really am beginning to think I am okay with it.

The vase and scissors are dropped off and now that I am beyond late, I trim the rose stems down, put water in the glass vase and put the roses in as fast as I can. I place the vase on the table and, at the last second, decide to also put the note from Alexander with it.

I take a photo of the roses and note, and send it to him, then another of me wearing the locket. Then I send a message to Alisha to let her know I'm leaving for the club.

I rush to get my boots on, collect my purse and stuff it with my phone, key card and a little black cardigan for the walk back.

***

The club is deafeningly loud with some song I don't recognise. The beat of it travels through the floor. Every thud of it carries right through me. It's bustling with a mix of people in all different versions of dressed up. Some pretty close to my effort level, and others in full costumes, masks and face paint. I get shoulder-checked by a Batman as he walks past me. He calls out to someone, and a table of people cheer and call out to *Batman*.

I spot one single empty stool at the bar between a group of girls who look like they are celebrating something and a guy in a pair of blue jeans, a ripped-up black button-up and some lazily done green face paint that I think is supposed to be a zombie. I decide that's where I'm going to wait for Alisha. It should make it easier for her to find me. I send her a message letting her know I am here and sitting at the bar. While waiting for her to reply, I decide to check in quickly on my emails, hoping there is something from any of the jobs I have applied for. I have no such luck; it's nothing but spam emails. Store advertisements and one from IN-SPIRE regarding me quitting. I decide to close my emails and deal with whatever they want later, much later. It does make me remember that I should probably check in with Nicki. I should have far sooner than this, and the realisation that I have completely left her in the cold hits me like a punch in the gut. I send her a message apologising for not contacting her sooner, and as soon as I get the chance, I will call her.

One of the girls from the group next to me calls out, "I'm getting married bitches!" I smile to myself. It's chaos. I need a drink. The music is ringing in my ears, and somehow the buzzing sound of people talking is louder than the music, but something about it is nice. It's hard to think amongst it all, and that's exactly what I need right now. I look around, hoping to spot Alisha. Maybe she is already here, and that's why she hasn't seen my message. I can barely make out anyone specific amongst the sea of people dancing, talking and drinking. With a sigh, I give up and turn back to the bar.

I inspect various bottles of alcohol lining the mirrored wall behind the bar. There are some bottles that are beautiful, intricate shapes that look more like decorative pieces than bottles.

"Are you waiting?" a skeleton in a costume and face paint with shoulder-length curly hair asks.

"A screwdriver please."

"No worries." He responds, then gets to work pouring my drink.

While I wait, I check my phone for a response from Alisha but there is still nothing. My anxiety is beginning to build. The idea of being in here completely alone is making me feel sick to my stomach. I toy with the idea of asking Alexander to meet me here, but squash it away. I can't ask him to travel nearly an hour to meet me here when surely Alisha will be here far before then anyway. I hover over the message from Alexander containing Logan's number. He is obviously going to be much closer to me than Alexander is. I know our interactions have been few and far between, and we have barely even said hello to each other, although after what Alexander and I did in the car, I'm not sure that even matters at this point. No. Stop it. I am an adult, damn it; I don't need someone to come rescue me from being alone. I like being alone, not particularly in a building full of people, but still. I'm overthinking again. Alisha will be here before I know it. I take a drink of my screwdriver. The combination of freshness from the orange juice and slight burn from the vodka is a pleasing combination. I accidentally finish it surprisingly fast. I should know better by now than to quench my nerves with alcohol. I have no desire to feel as rubbish as I did the other night. Nonetheless, I wave the bartender down and order another. I check my phone once more. This time, a little tick signifying that Alisha has read my message is there. I let my shoulders slump with relief and down my drink. She hasn't replied yet, but at least I know she knows I am here, like she asked, and she should be able to find me.

I finish the second drink and decide to wait until Alisha gets here before ordering a third. I get the sudden urge to pee. Once again, I look at my phone. I'm growing desperate now. There is still nothing. I gaze through the clusters of people one final time with no luck. I slump against the bar and motion to the bartender that I would like to order another screwdriver. The air around me is still. Every hair on my body stands on end. Every inch of my skin is buzzing as if someone in this room is watching me.

The feeling makes my stomach turn. I turn back towards the bar to pay for my drink and catch a glimpse of the ghost of myself that is in the reflection in the mirror behind the bar. I down my drink once more, hoping to find the confidence to work out who exactly it is who I can feel watching me.

I get off the stool and make my way through the sea of people, taking the time to look at everyone I possibly can. There are groups of people in booths talking and laughing amongst themselves, others are dancing, sitting at the bar, walking around. Everyone appears to be wrapped up in their own space. Even the people who are alone are seemingly focused on anything but me. With every step further I take from the bar, the feeling still doesn't seem to relent. I decide I'm done. If I don't leave now, I'm going to throw up all over the floor and the poor group of people around me. The chill of the night air hits as soon as I step out of the door. To my dismay, it makes my stomach bubble and flip rather than better. That's it, I'm done. I will meet up with Alisha and come back here, but I'm not waiting here for her. We can meet at the apartment. I send her a message telling her there has been a change of plans, and I will meet her at our room. Something in me is screaming to turn around. The feeling on my back that someone is right there, so very close to touching me, is so prominent it almost burns. Against every other instinct I have, I turn. I lock eyes with someone in a pair of black jeans, a black hoodie and a doll mask. I can't make out anything about them besides them being maybe a little taller than me. I watch as, ever so slowly, whoever it is raises their hand and waves at me. I turn back out of the bar and beeline it for the four blocks towards the room. My stomach is hating every single step. I try my best not to focus on it and just get back, but the footsteps echoing from behind me, growing ever closer, don't allow me the luxury of stopping. They seem to be matching me step by step, and with my heart pounding, I round the corner to my apart-ment. I fumble my key card out of my bag, but don't stop running until I reach the doors of the hotel.

Fifteen

I step out of the elevator and take a few steps toward my door. I stop myself before unlocking it. My blood is boiling, and my skin is itchy with anxiety. It's not possible, but I still feel like I'm being watched. There is a ding behind me. The sudden, unexpected sound makes my heart lurch through my chest. The doors open, and in a split second, I make the decision. For once in my life, I'm not going to be a coward, I'm not going to second-guess myself. I reach for my car keys in my bag and position my house key between my first two fingers and form a fist around the rest of the keys. I turn to face my stalker with my fist at the ready. A man steps through the elevator. I am eye level with his tie and crisp white shirt.

I draw my fist back and, in a flash, drive it towards him as he approaches. His hand connects with the side of my wrist. He turns me so my back is against him, and he holds my arm in place across my body.'

"Let me the fuck go!"

"Miss Locket, stop. It's me."

Fuck.

"Logan. Why the fuck are you following me?" I struggle against him, and he lets me free.

"I saw you leave the club. I'm just making sure everything is okay."

"Everything is fine." I snap and leave him standing in the corridor and go into my room.

All the air is punched out of my lungs. It takes a few seconds for my brain to catch up with what my eyes are seeing. The room is in ruins. The bedding is thrown everywhere, my belongings are strewn across the bedroom, kitchen and dining area. The vase containing the flowers from Alexander is shattered all over the floor. I walk further into the room, and through the open door of the bathroom, I can see the word SLUT written in what looks like my lipstick on the mirror. The sink and floor are littered with my makeup.

I'm shaking so much it verges on painful. My knees threaten to buckle out from under me, but by some miracle, I manage to find the ability to get myself back out of the room. Logan is standing right by my door, looking toward the elevator. Just as he was when he was standing out the front of Alexander's room. If I didn't need him right now, I would be inclined to chew him out for it.

"Logan. . . someone. . . my room. . . It's" I can't seem to manage to get a single word out, but somehow, he seems to decipher enough to know to rip the key card from my hand and go into my room. As if I'm on autopilot, my feet move, following behind him.

I watch as he looks around the room, examining the damage. He grabs a glass from the sink and fills it with water.

"Sit and drink this." He pulls one of the dining room chairs out for me.

"I need air." I rasp. He groans frustratingly but leads me toward the balcony doors. He waits for me to sit on one of the seats before passing me the glass.

"Don't move." His voice is stern and full of warning, but his eyes are soft.

"Please don't leave me alone," I whisper.

"I will leave the balcony door open; I will just be inside. I need to make a call.

I manage to choke out an okay. And watch him go back into the crime scene of a hotel room.

"Mr Truette, there has been an incident at Miss Locket's apartment." There is a pause, and angry, muffled shouting coming through the other end of the phone. "She seems fine, Sir." . . . "You want to keep it internal?" . . . "Yes, of course, I will make the arrangements as soon as she's brought to you."

Everything else he says becomes muffled background noise behind the screaming in my mind. Go to him? Is he talking about taking me to Alexander? What about Alisha? I need to call her. I can't let her walk into this. We need to call the police and get this cleaned up.

"Miss Locket, we need to go. I will pack your things for you. Please just tell me what you need."

"Logan, we can't go anywhere. We need to call the police. We need to make arrangements for my friend. She flew in tonight and is supposed to be staying here with me."

He begins rushing around the room, throwing my clothes into my suitcase. "It is being handled, Miss Locket, but for now, mine and Mr Truette's priority is your safety."

I don't have the energy to argue, and to be honest, the idea of being wrapped up with Alexander and far away from this hotel room sounds like exactly what I need right now.

I wrap my arms around myself as a tear escapes me. The reality of my night seems to be sinking in.

"Miss Locket. Is there anything specific you need me to pack for you?"

"No, Logan, what you have already done is enough. Can we please just leave?" My voice is meek. He looks up at me, and the sight of me seems to give him pause. He makes quick work of zipping up my suitcase. He carries it to me and drops it at our feet. He places his hands on my shoulders and locks his eyes to mine. I look at him, and the ocean is seemingly looking back.

"Miss Locket, I will make sure you are safe. I will get you to Mr Truette's home, where he is waiting for you. I will personally make arrangements for your friend, and I will personally find out who was in this room. I promise you, you are safe now, and everything will be okay."

My chest tightens with every word. His jaw is tense, but his eyes are so kind and soft.

"I'm so sorry, Logan," I whisper.

"Miss?" he asks, raising his eyebrow at me.

"I have been so cold toward you, and at no point have you been deserving of it. I'm not used to someone watching my every move, but right now I couldn't be more grateful that you were."

"There have been no hard feelings, Miss Locket. Come, Mr Truette is waiting." He picks my suitcase back up and ushers me to leave the room first. I grab my bag on the way out, and for what I hope won't be the last time, I leave the room.

In the elevator, I try to call Alisha. I curse out loud, I fight the urge to lunge my phone across the elevator.

"I will ensure she is fine, Miss Locket. As soon as we get in the car downstairs, I will have people on it."

"Thank you," I whisper, but still decide to send her a message.

Me: Alisha, something has happened
With our room. You can't stay
Tonight, please call me asap.

I can't help the sinking feeling that this message was for nothing. The elevator reaches the lobby, and Logan wastes no time getting me and my belongings loaded into the car.

My phone rings and I can't help the small smile that hits my lips when I see Alexanders name on my screen.

"Hey baby. How are you doing?" his voice is unusually soft and sounds so unexpectedly different over the phone.

"Alexander." I choke out. It's all I can manage before the tears become uncontrollable and the burning in my throat turn into full-blown sobs.

"Oh, Sam, I am so sorry. I never should have let you insist on staying there. I knew there was always the risk of something happening, but I never imagined something like this."

"It's okay, Alexander. This isn't your fault."

I'm so embarrassed in myself crying through the phone to him.

"Alexander, I'm so tired, I'm going to try to rest while I'm in the car. I will see you soon."

"Are you sure?"

"Yeah, I'm sure."

He says goodbye, but he sounds reluctant. We hang up, and I tighten my arms around myself and let my anvil eyelids weigh down. I fall asleep to the sound of Logan making phone call after phone call.

Sixteen

Logan leads me through a set of massive mahogany double doors. They open into a foyer bigger than my lounge room. Its walls are lined with paintings of a mist-filled forest. All five of them seem to flow off each other, creating one large painting if they were put together. The one in the centre holds a lonely cabin with the gentle glow of a fire shining from its windows. It's beautiful. Footsteps approach quickly from the left of us, and I turn to see Alexander coming into view from what looks to be a sitting room with a matching pair of white sofas, a natural slab coffee table and an exposed brick wall lining the back of the room. It sticks out in contrast to the off-white walls surrounding it. We lock eyes, and he appears to drop his shoulders and let out a sigh.

"I will be in my office." Logan says, there is no softness in his voice now, but when he turns back to look at me before leaving through the archway directly in front of us, he gives me a small, reassuring smile.

"Thank you, Logan," I say quietly. He nods, then is out of view.

Alexander's arms are around my waist. He is crushing me against him so hard it almost hurts. Any other time, I think I would try to push away, but right now, I melt into him and accept the air being crushed from my lungs.

"It's nice to see you have decided to start being nice to my staff." A smile tugs at his lips, but worry lines still remain around his eyes.

"I think I would be nice to any big, strong man who is promising to keep me safe." I flutter my eyelashes and look up at him through them.

He shakes his head and squeezes tighter. Unfortunately, I think I've reached my limit. I push out of his grasp. He hesitates at first, then lets me go.

He lifts the locket from my neck and turns it over in his hand. He seems to attempt to hide his smile but fails.

"I'm so sorry about tonight. This never should have happened." He looks me over, and for the first time, there isn't a hint of hunger in him, just concern.

Tears pool at my eyelids. I can't really pinpoint why the hot ball in my throat or the tightening in my chest has started. It could be because I'm not used to someone showing me such care, or perhaps it's all of the events from tonight. My stalker, my hotel, my worry for Alisha. Whatever it is, it's winning, and as the tears start to stream, my body trembles.

Shit. His arm is around my waist, and he is leading me through a different door from the one Logan had walked through to the right. We pass through an oversized open-plan kitchen and dining. There is more exposed brick flowing through. He doesn't leave me much time to look around, but I catch a glimpse of more paintings and huge windows that seem to surround an indoor greenhouse.

He continues upstairs into a hallway lined with various doors. He takes us through one at the very end. It's a dimly lit bedroom. The city lights twinkle through sheer curtains that cover the floor-to-ceiling windows lining the entire back and side walls. The room is scarcely filled with just a king bed, a matching set of side tables and a black leather armchair that faces the bed. I hesitate when it looks like he is going to lead us towards the bed. I want him, but not right now, not when I can't string a cohesive thought together outside of my worry for Alisha.

"We aren't going to bed. As much as I would love nothing more than to clear your head and think of nothing but me and the things I'm doing to you.

It will have to wait." He gives my hand a reassuring squeeze, but it does little to calm the hammering in my chest.

He continues through to a door to the left of the room. It opens to a bathroom that continues the flow of the windows outside. A two-person shower is to the right, both sides holding two separate shower heads on each. It looks like it's made of concrete; the adjoining two walls that aren't made up of massive windows are also concrete. The room is warm from the heating lamps. I hadn't noticed I was cold until a shiver of warmth travels through me.

He lets go of my hand and leaves me in place while he begins to fill the round free-standing bath. It looks big enough to comfortably fit three people.

He adds something to the water. I can't see the bottle, but the room fills with the smell of lavender. I inhale deeply and tightly wrap my arms around myself. The bath continues to fill, and steam fills the room. Alexander saunters towards me, unbuttoning his black shirt as he does. My mind splits into a chaotic, confused mess of wanting him but not wanting to be seen right now. Of wanting to be in that bath, letting the water consume every part of me, every thought, every worry. But also wanting him to be the one to do that exact same thing.

"Join me?" his words are as soft as silk, yet they manage to smash down the wall of anxiety bubbling through me. I manage nothing more than a small nod. I'm afraid that if I try to speak right now, I will cry again.

He kisses me, it's gentle, it's careful, and it's over far too soon.

His hands find the bottom of my shirt. He glides his hands along my skin under my shirt at a leisurely pace. He moves them back down and hooks under my shirt, lifting it over my head.

He follows quickly with my skirt. He raises an eyebrow and smirks. "Giving me a glimpse into the real you, I see." Heat rises to my cheeks as I realise he is talking about my cotton underwear that I had specifically chosen, one, for comfort, but two, because I was sure no one, especially Alexander, would see them.

I brace my arms on his shoulders to steady myself while he removes them.

"Shall we keep the boots on?" he steps back and looks me up and down. Instinctively, I move my arms to cover myself.

"Oh no, Sam, there will be none of that." His voice turns to gravel. Part of me is uncomfortable with the way he thinks he can tell me I can't cover myself up, but a bigger, bolder part of me takes a steadying breath, moves my hands back to my side and squares my shoulders back.

"Good girl." My stomach tightens, and he removes my boots.

He holds my hand to support me as I step into the bath. I sit with my back to one side, and quickly he joins me, sitting on the other. I do my best to remain polite and avert my gaze from everywhere but his face. He picks up my left foot and rests it on his outstretched leg. He picks up a bottle from the shelf behind him and puts some of the oil from inside on his hand. He picks my foot back up and begins working the oil over my skin. His touch is pushing on painful, yet an appreciative moan slips through. I close my eyes and let myself sink further into the water, letting myself relish in this impossible moment. I'm in a beautiful house, naked in a bath with a billionaire who is rubbing my feet like he does it as a profession.

As soon as he stops, reality crashes into me, and my chest tightens so hard I feel like every rib is going to crash under its weight.

He picks up the other foot, and I let him, but I can't continue to sit here in silence.

"I need to know that my friend is okay."

"Logan is working on finding her for you."

I pull my foot from his grasp and sit up. "He doesn't even know her name."

He laughs, and it makes the water lap around us. "He has found far more with far less. However, he has her name. he got it from reception at the hotel."

My mouth opens and closes as I fumble over my next words.

"That's not legal, Alexander. It's a huge breach in confidentiality."

His jaw tightens and smirks, not in a way I have seen him do before. This is cocky.

"Some circumstances, like your life being in danger and perhaps even your friend, allow for a little rule-breaking." He shrugs. He seems to be eyeing me cautiously, as if he is waiting to see how I will react.

"Huh." Is all I can manage in response. What else am I supposed to say when he is sitting across from me, admitting that he has the power to get away with breaking confidentiality? How much further does it go?

"There is nothing more you can do right now. Logan and other members of my security team are tracking your friend down, arranging accommodation for her and making sure she is safe. As soon as I get updated from Logan that she has been found and made safe, I will tell you."

I hate it, but he's right. I'm not even in the same city as her anymore. The best I could do is make some phone calls to track her down, but I wouldn't be surprised if that is the first thing Logan already did.

"Come here." He opens his arms, and I do as he says. "Turn around." His voice is back to being soft, and with no hesitation, I oblige.

He positions me so my head is against his shoulder and my back is against his chest. He grabs a washcloth and soap from the shelf and, ever so slowly, works the soap-covered cloth over my body. Starting with my arms, then moving to my breast, and down my stomach. I close my eyes again and allow every sensation to take over. The warm cloth, the dripping water, his fingers. There is a hum in his chest as my nipples harden under his touch.

The day is catching up with me again, and fatigue washes over me. I sink into him more.

"We need to get out now, baby, wake up"

"Hmm?"

He kisses the top of my head and runs his fingers through my hair.

Oh shit, I fell asleep. I sit up, mortified. I move too fast, and bath water sloshes over the side of the bath.

"I am so sorry, I didn't realise how tired I was."

"I'm not sure it's just because you're tired. It's been an interesting evening, to say the least. Why didn't you tell me about the stalker at the club?"

My mouth once again falls open.

"How did you?" he cuts me off.

"Logan got the security footage. He told me he had to follow you from the club back to the hotel. It only shows the back of whoever it was. What did they look like?"

"I don't know, they were wearing a mask."

His only response is a distracted nod.

"Come, the water is getting cold, and there is something we need to do."

We get out, and he wraps a towel around me.

"I have a way to make this all go away, just for a little while. For the rest of tonight, I don't want you to worry about your friend, about yourself or our stalker. I want every single thought you have to be consumed by me. But you have to be willing to trust me."

"I trust you." I breathe, I think, surprising both of us. I have no clue in the world what the hell he intends to do. Get me drunk? Take me to bed with him? No matter the option, I am down for it because the truth is, I do want to forget. At least for right now.

"Oh, my little siren." His eyes darken, and heat travels through every delicious part of me.

Seventeen

Relief washes over me as Alexander reads out a message he got from Logan, informing him they have found Alisha and set her up at a different hotel with a member of Alexander's security keeping watch at her new hotel. She also wanted me to know she had lost her phone somewhere after disembarking the plane.

My whole nervous system seems to take a breath knowing Alisha is okay.

The smell of cedar wood surrounds us. The dimly lit room Alexander took us into, which sits along the hallway down from his bedroom, looks like a smaller version of the master. The city's view twinkles its lights in a brilliant display that mutes through the sheer curtains, which can be compared to the night sky. The only difference is this room has chests of drawers, three large ones sitting along the wall opposite the window, and the bed has pillows with a matching deep blue satin sheet instead of a chair facing the bed. There is a matching sofa.

The air feels different. It's thick with unspoken desires and anticipation. The sound of the door clicking shut behind me makes icy darts hit my chest. I tense as his footsteps approach.

"Drop the towel and stand by the bed, facing the sofa."

This time, I allow myself to hesitate. "Why?"

He comes out from behind me and traces his thumb over my bottom lip. He pushes his thumb in just enough that it sits between my teeth, and in a moment of boldness a bite it. His eyes widen in shock, but just as quickly, it is replaced with pure greed. He moves his hand, instead putting it under my chin and lifting it so I have to look him in the eyes.

"Because, Samantha, I am going to take every one of your thoughts. You spend so much time overthinking, and if you will allow me to, I'm going to teach you how to shove your worries away. There is no need to think twice, to question or to worry. In this room with me, all you need to do is say yes. To everything. That's your only thought."

What the fuck? This is what he's into? He wants to dominate me. Our conversation in the restaurant echoes in my mind. *I enjoy being the one in control, not the one just along for the ride.* He wasn't talking about sailing or flying. The icy daggers turn into full-on boulders, but the tightening deep in the pit of my stomach is intense and hot and writhing with anticipation.

"You want to dominate me?" My words come out breathy, and I can't tell if it's from anxiety or desire.

"I want you to want me to."

Flashes of his mouth on me, his tongue, of him inside me all play out in my mind in snapshots so quickly I'm dizzy. Twice he tied my hands, every time his words were commanding, him shutting it down and making me eat. Little signs have been here every time, and every time, I loved every delicious second of it.

"Will you hurt me?" The question is word vomit and out before I can hide my fear.

"No, Samantha, I have no intentions of hurting you. I would never push you beyond what I know you're capable of."

Some of the ice seemingly melts away.

"If you want to stop at any point, just say. I will not force you into anything, just encourage you to do what is asked of you."

The ice is gone as I look into the brown gold flecked eyes of the man I have come to grow so stupidly trusting of over the last few days. My curiosity and desire are winning any pathetic attempt of reservation that is remaining. I step back from him, drop my towel at my feet and walk as confidently as I can to the bed. I do as he said and face the sofa.

"Kneel." Raise my eyebrow at him, but do as I'm told.

He crosses the room to one of the sets of drawers. He opens and closes multiple of them and tosses items from each on the bed. I fight the urge to look at what he is getting out. I don't want my fear of what's to come to get in the way of what's to come.

He finishes up with what he is doing, and I watch as he sits leisurely on the sofa in front of me.

"Crawl to me, little siren." His voice is gravel, and his eyes are dark in that way that makes heat travel up my spine and spread through every cell inside me, and it's in this moment that I realise all it would take is for this man to look at me just as he is now. Like his universe would tilt out of place if I was to walk away and say no, and I would crawl through hot coals if that's what he asked of me. It's a terrifying realisation, but more than that, I'm terrified that when I look at him, that's exactly how I feel too.

I do as I'm told and crawl along the wood floor. He shifts in his seat, and through his towel, I can see the effect the sight of me is having on him. I should feel degraded, ashamed, but more than anything, I feel a wicked sense of power.

I sit back up on my knees once I reach him.

"You are a sight indeed, my little siren." His words work just as well as his damn hands.

"You're flushed, Miss Locket. I wonder if perhaps you are already ready for me?"

He lifts his hand and moves his finger in a come-hither motion. I do as he says and get to my feet. He removes the towel from around his waist. My breath hitches as I drink in the sight of him.

"Put your legs on either side of me." He commands.

I plunge my teeth into my bottom lip as a wicked idea crosses my mind. I flash him a smile and drop back down to my knees.

"Samantha." My name is said as a warning. I put my hands on either of his thighs to brace myself.

"I told you to." . . . My mouth is on him, sucking as much of him down as I can. His words are cut off and replaced with a gasp. I fight the urge to giggle and instead lightly drag my teeth from his base to the tip.

He sucks in a breath through clenched teeth. I take in as much of him as I can again, getting as close to his base as possible, this time dragging my tongue along the bottom of him on the way back up. Once I reach the tip, I flick my tongue over the slit at the end.

"Fuck, Sam." His hands find my hair, and he collects it all into one hand, twists it around his wrist and pulls. I fight against him and wrap my lips back around him. He relents on the pulling, allowing me to continue my torturous, slow teasing. I alternate between teeth and tongue.

An appreciative hum comes from somewhere deep in his chest, and I pick up the pace. He begins thrusting, meeting my pace. I do my best to relax, allowing him to go deeper. He sucks in another sharp breath, and his body begins to still. I look up at him through my lashes and watch as his eyebrow raises. He is asking permission again, or just curious to see what I will do. I'm not sure which it is right now. He lets go of my head and lets me have complete control again. I continue sucking him down, going lower every time. I circle his tip with my tongue, watch as his fists clench at his side.

"Samantha!" My name is a warning again, and it's all the incentive I need to wrap my lips around him one final time and bite down with just enough pressure to make him moan ever so deliciously as he empties himself into the back of my throat.

I stand back up without a word. His eyes are wide and lust-filled. I expect him to say something or to pull me down onto him, but instead he gets to his feet and stands in front of me. He puts his hand on the back of my throat. It doesn't hurt, but I am certainly held firmly in place. Every pulse point in my body is hammering with anticipation. He tilts my head up, and we connect. His tongue is in my mouth, greedily exploring. I take his desperate need and show him just how much I need him too. I suck his bottom lip in and bite it. I didn't think it was possible, but he deepens the kiss more. Pressure and heat build, every thought turns to a blur, there is just him and me and the need to have him touch me, to be in me.

"Alexander please." I moan against him.

"Not until you promise me that from now on you will do as you are told." I can't, I know it will be an empty promise and part of me wants to see what will happen if I tell him no, unless of course that means he won't touch me at all. I can't risk it. I need him now.

"I promise." I whimper.

He abruptly stops the kiss. "Go stand by the bed." I waste no time doing as he says. Trying my best to hide just how giddy with excitement I am.

I finally get a look at what he put on the bed earlier. Rope, what looks to be a vibrator, lube, a plug, and a condom. I gasp at the sight of it all. I've never used a vibrator, and I've most certainly never used a plug.

"Get on the bed." Something much stronger than fear puts my feet on autopilot. I lay on the bed and watch him pick up the two spools of thin red rope. There are little circles on the wood of the bed, one at each corner. He opens the two at the top of the bed, revealing little golden rings. He loops the rope around them and knots the other end of the rope around my wrists. He gives them both a tug, and once he is satisfied that I am firmly in place and unable to escape whatever is to come, he gives a small, satisfied nod.

"I need you to remember that you can tell me to stop."

I'm not confident in my ability to form words right now, so I nod.

"Good." He goes back over to the drawers and picks up a remote from the top of it. He presses a few buttons, and the room fills with the same entrancing music that was playing in the car on the way to the boat.

"I noticed you liked it." He shrugs, and if I'm not mistaken, looks a little embarrassed at the admission of noticing.

"I found it wonderful." By some miracle, I manage to speak loud enough to be heard.

He joins me on the bed. Positioning himself between my legs and hovering his face over my breast. His breath is cool against my skin. I push my chest up, longing for him to touch me properly.

"You're an impatient one, Miss Locket, something I look forward to helping you improve on."

"Please. Touch me." I plead, pushing my chest up again and pulling against my restraints.

He grins but gives in to me. His tongue flicks over my nipple. I watch in a mix of awe and desire as he bites down. Shock ripples through me. I gasp at the unexpected pain. He moves to the next one, repeating the same process. Biting down and making me cry out, then sucking and licking before I have time to feel it properly.

I thrust my hips up towards him, and he places his hand on my hip and pins me back into place.

"I can't remember the last time I had to fuck my own hand. But you, *my little siren.* You have made me a very desperate man. I could think of nothing else last night but all the things I planned to do with you in this room. So now, you're going to feel just a taste of the pain I felt when you left me needing."

His lips are on mine, stealing my words before I get a chance to say anything.

His hand moves from my hip and finds my clit. He begins circling so tortuously slow. I move against him, urging him to give me more.

He moves his fingers lower, and a smile crosses his lips.

"Oh, Miss Locket. If only I could ensure you were always this ready for me. So I can take you whenever I feel the need."

He plunges two fingers inside, and I gasp. He palms my clit and removes the reinserts his fingers, building up in pace and hitting my clit just right. I pull tight against my restraints and cry out as he brings me close to the edge. "Alexander." I try to tell him I need him to keep going, but words fail beyond his name.

"Not yet, you don't." he pulls his fingers out, and I hate myself. I am so overwhelmed. Hot, cold, sore, pleasure, need. He grabs the small bullet-shaped vibrator from beside us and turns it on. He places it against my clit, and I cry out again.

He leans over and, with one hand, manages to untie the knot around my right hand.

"Hold it in place." He says and replaces his hand with mine.

I do as he says while trying to watch what he is doing next, but waves of pleasure radiate through me. It's too much, it's not enough. I close my eyes and let myself feel everything. I vaguely make out the sound of a bottle being opened, and I'm pretty sure I know why. I've never done anything like this before, but right now I can't imagine anything hotter with anyone else. I want him, in every possible way.

"Fold your legs up so your knees are bent at your chest."

I do as he says, but choose to keep my eyes shut. As much as I want what is about to happen, I don't want to see.

Alexander sucks in a breath. "You are such a sight, Samantha."

Another wave of pleasure steals my words from me, and I can offer no more than a moan in response. Cold liquid runs down me, and I tense at the unexpected and unfamiliar feeling. The familiar sound of a foil packet being torn makes my stomach tighten. *Holy shit.* I feel his weight pressing down on the bed on either side of me. I finally open my eyes. He is hovering just over me, the sight of him looking at me like he is starving almost tips me over the edge.

"Breathe, Samantha."

As soon as I do, he is pressing the plug against my arse. Ever so slowly, he applies pressure. It's forbidden, it's new, it's *so fucking hot*.

"That's it, good girl." He is talking through clenched teeth.

He gets it all the way in, and before I get a chance to get used to the sensation, he is inside me. Nothing about him is gentle this time. Over and over, he thrusts into me, drawing himself in deeper. I cry out a garbled version of his name as the pressure finally relents and I let go, tensing around him. I toss the vibrator to the side and hold my legs in place, watching as he continues to thrust greedily into me.

He stills and finds his release. I let go of my legs and instead wrap them around him, trapping him in place.

He smiles and shakes his head at me a little and plants a chaste kiss on the top of my head.

I untangle from him, and he withdraws from me. I wince at the unfamiliar feeling of the plug being removed. He gets off the bed and puts everything that was used into a little container and places it on the top of the drawers.

I stretch out my limbs, testing how bad the pain is now that the high of it all is wearing off. There is definitely some soreness in more places than one, but it's bearable.

"I'm tempted to leave you like this, tied to the bed. At least this way I will know you're safe."

I'm *pretty sure* he is joking, but there is something behind his eyes, something dark and worry-filled that makes me not so sure.

"I'm joking, Sam." He reassures me and unties my wrist. Damn my inability to hide my thoughts behind my expressions.

"Come, shower with me."

I take his hand and let him lead me, both of us still completely naked, down the hall and back to his bathroom.

Eighteen

The warmth from the flames that flicker in the fireplace licks at my skin. I pull the throw rug over my legs from the back of the sofa. Alexander had encouraged me to read whatever I would like while waiting for him in his library until he finished tending to some work in his office.

I browsed the book, of course, but I just don't feel right about touching his belongings. I instead decide to continue one of the eBooks on my phone. I open the last book I was reading, but after five attempts of just re-reading the same line over and over again, I give up. I instead check in on my job applications, clean out my spam emails and go through any new ones. Once I too quickly finish up with that, I move on to checking in with my mother.

I contemplate sending her a generic message letting her know I'm okay and having a great holiday. It's not a complete lie, and really, what else am I supposed to say? Alisha isn't with me. I met a billionaire, and his ex may or may not be stalking me. Oh, and now I'm at the billionaire's house in a completely different city because my hotel room was trashed?

I decide instead to call her, my mind in a mess, and right now I think the best thing for me is to hear her voice. She picks up on the second ring. Her soft, ever-frail, growing voice comes through the phone, and it causes the complete opposite response than I was hoping.

"Hi, darling." Tears welled in my eyes.

"Hi mum." *Shit, my voice is too shaky.* I clear my throat and try again. "How are you and Dad?"

"I am well, your father is under the weather, but if he actually takes his meds for once and gets some rest, he will be fine. How are you and Alisha enjoying your time away?"

I can't mess this up; I can't let her hear through my lies. This was a mistake. She always knows. I do my best to try anyway. There is no sense in worrying both of them with any of this.

"We are having the best time. It's all beaches, shopping and good food. It's exactly what we both needed."

"What's happened, Sammie?"

Damn this woman.

"Nothing that's a problem; it's just a funny story I can tell you when we get back."

She's not going to let this go. I should have just messaged her like I was going to.

"Mum, I have to go, we were getting ready to go out, I just wanted to quickly check in." She is reluctant but ultimately ends the call.

Alexander is still not back, the idea of going to search for him is tempting. His house, although warm in the literal sense, feels cold. It's lonely and quiet. It makes me miss my farmhouse. I knew I would hit a point during this holiday where being homesick would knock me down, but never had I imagined it would hit me while lounging on the sofa in a private library in the most beautiful house I have ever stepped foot in.

I attempt again to read. Although it didn't seem like it, talking with mum seems to have helped at least a little because this time I find I am able to read.

***

A huge bang sound echoes around my tired mind. I jolt awake, my heart is racing and sweat lines the back of my neck. The room is almost pitch black, besides the gentle glow from the now almost completely burned-out fire. Use the torch on my phone to try to locate a light switch. Once I do, I notice that the door into the library I had left open is now closed. *Something woke you up.* I consider the sound that startled me was perhaps Alexander closing the door, but it seems unlikely, unless it was slammed. Unease washes over me. I want to go find him, but I don't feel exactly comfortable stalking around his house in the dark. I check the time, and to my surprise, it's four AM. He left me to sleep in here. I figured I had drifted off for an hour, and he perhaps left me while he was still working.

I take an unsteady breath. *Don't be a coward.* I open the door and do my best to make my way through the house using only the light from the now open doorway of the library and my phone torch.

I pass by the kitchen island and notice a note with my name on it. The handwriting is immediately familiar. I unfold the in half paper.

Good morning, little Siren. I have gone for an early morning run. I was tempted to ask you to join me, but I couldn't bring myself to disturb you. If I'm not back before you wake up, please help yourself to the kitchen. You were asleep by the time I came to get you for dinner. You must eat, Samantha. - Your Alexander.

I re-read the last line of the note more times than I would ever be willing to admit out loud. He is such a confusing mix of demanding and generous. This constant stake of whiplash he has me in is going to make me break out in hives or something.

Your Alexander. The words circle around in my mind, and a dumb, face-splitting grin crosses my face. This impossible man with the world at his feet and desires far darker than I could ever expect, who could have any magazine cover woman he wanted to hand-pick, is calling himself mine. *It hasn't even been a week.* Logic and reason claw up my spine, trying their best to knock me back down to reality. The problem is, I know this is insane, I know the things I let him to last night are something I don't think I could ever see myself letting someone else ever do. Letting him command me in such ways, letting him do things to my body that, before last night, I was repulsed by. I know nothing about him, and it seems every time I learn something new, it's something that should have me running for the hills. He even tried to warn me away, and yet, here I am, standing in his kitchen with no more than one of his dress shirts on and the desire to have him hurry up and get back so he can bend me over this kitchen island.

For what feels like the millionth time this week, I shake my head at myself and the absurdity of myself, whoever the hell it is I seem to be becoming because of him and this whole damn ridiculous situation.

I fold the note up and put it back in place. I look around the kitchen and the living room. Now that my eyes have adjusted, the city lights from across the river are lighting up the space just enough that I can walk around without tripping over or bumping into anything. I open the door and step out onto the balcony. The early morning air is freezing, but the city view is breathtaking.

I walk over to the huge windows facing the city and pull one of the thin sheer curtains to the side. It reveals a handle on one of the huge pains, and I realise now that I am up close that it's a door that leads out to a balcony.

Icy wind rips through my hair and pierces the skin of my bare legs. I wrap my arms around myself in a futile attempt to stay outside. A door closes from somewhere behind me, and for the second time this morning, I startle at the unexpected sound. I figure it must be Alexander returning from his run. I go back inside in search of him.

I find my way back to the front door, but even in the almost complete darkness, it's obvious that no one is there. If he had of come through the house already, we would have passed each other. I turn, looking through the arched doorway to my right. I hadn't taken much notice of this room when Logan had left through it last night. There is a bar sitting towards the back of the room, more paintings on the wall, two sofas, a handful of armchairs and a pool table all laid. But none of the silhouettes that make up that room are what catch my attention.

There is a door to the left, slightly ajar. A dim orange glow bleeds through the doorway. Perhaps Alexander's office is also through this way, and he went straight into here when returning home.

I knock on the door, but there is no response. I pinch my bottom lip between my thumb and finger and contemplate between leaving and waiting for him to be finished in there or just walking in. I don't want to interrupt if he is doing something important. *Coward.* I cringe in on myself for what I am about to do and hope that he doesn't consider it rude and get mad.

I push the door open. There is a massive desk with a laptop on and turned on, and an empty chair sitting at it.

I look around the room, there is no other way out of here. There are no windows in this room. The walls are lined with filing cabinets, bookshelves, and a sofa and coffee table sit next to the doorway.

What the fuck?

I step further into the room. A pile of something on the floor between the chair and the desk catches my attention. I strain to make my eyes adjust. As soon as I do, I scream. Realising my mistake, I slam my hand over my mouth. It's not a pile, it's a man. He looks so similar to Logan, I think it's him at first.

I back out of the room, every part of me trembling and a panic attack building. The words *what the fuck* scream and repeat over and over, I can't seem to form any other thought.

I find myself back in the entryway. My breathing becomes heavy and painful, my throat dries, and my stomach is doing flips. *There was a fucking hole in his head.* The realisation buckles my knees. That's what woke me up. Whoever that was has been shot in the head. And whoever did it has to be who I heard using the door. My brain seems to connect back into place. I get to my feet and sprint to the library. I close the door behind me and immediately go to call Alexander, but stop myself. What if it was him? This is his home, and as far as I can tell, that was his office. Who the hell goes out for a run when it's still dark out? What if it was a lie, and actually, he just needed to make sure I thought he was some-where he isn't? I know absolutely nothing about this man. This powerful man who could quite easily get away with God knows what. I need a plan to get out. I consider calling Logan to come get me, but that's such a stupid idea; he works for Alexander, and if he is some sort of criminal capable of killing someone, I'm sure the man who is his security would know that.

My phone rings, and my heart bottoms out. I can't answer if it's Alexander. I wouldn't be able to keep calm. The number is unknown. I let it ring, hesitating. Until I remember that Alisha lost her phone, and she could be calling from a different number. I could tell her! We can figure this out together.

I answer the phone, but it's not Alisha's voice on the other end.

"Is this Samantha locket?" an unfamiliar voice asks.

"Yes, it is."

"Miss Locket, I am Doctor Powell from Grace-well Hospital. Your parents, Maverick and Sadie, were in a car accident. They are stable, but we need their next of kin to..." I cut him off.

"I am on my way. I am in a completely different state right now, but I will be on the first flight in. The dead body in the office is already being pushed to the back of my mind. I know it's fucked up. I know I should call the cops and report it, but I can't. I just. . . I can't. I need to get home. Now. *He's a monster.* A building, burning lump in my throat forms. I need to go, I will not let myself cry over a fucking murderer. He warned me, he fucking warned me that he didn't want us to happen. Obviously, for more reasons than just his Psychotic ex, assuming she even is psychotic. For all I know, none of it's true, and he is actually the insane one. The evidence certainly points to it.

I run towards the front door. Not daring to look to my left towards the office. I don't think I can stomach it.

There is a tightness forming around my throat. I feel like my airway is being closed off. I instinctively put my hand around my throat and feel the locket Alexander had given me. It suddenly feels like twenty kilos are pulling down on me. I rip the locket from my neck and toss it. I hear it land somewhere on the tiled floor behind me.

I don't care that I'm practically naked, I don't care that I have nothing but my phone on me. I run outside, I leave out Alexander's front gate, turn to the right and keep running. I don't stop until my bare feet are burning from running on the freezing pavement. I estimate that I am around eight blocks from his house. I pull my phone out, get my exact location and order a ride share to take me to the airport. While waiting for the driver, I book my flight. There is one leaving two hours from now. It's longer than I would have liked to wait, but it will have to do.

Nineteen

I arrive at home just long enough to get my car keys, get in the car and do my best to weave across town through traffic and get to the hospital. A small part of me wishes I had quickly ducked inside and changed out of Alexander's shirt, but I have wasted enough time stopping to get my own car as it is. Thank God for the clothing store in the airport where I managed to find a pair of denim shorts and thongs. The drive is thankfully not too bad. By some miracle, I have managed to get into town just before the late afternoon traffic starts.

I find a park only a block away from the hospital. I run the whole way to the emergency room and burst through the doors. I don't stop running until I get to the triage desk.

"I'm here to see Mr and Mrs Locket." The woman behind the counter with fiery curly hair looks up over her glasses and gives me a warm smile.

"Sure, darlin', let me look them up for you. You got a first name for them?"

I tell her their names and confirm my identification. She types, pauses, looks at the screen with a frown, then types again. place my hand on my hip and tap my fingers impatiently.

"I'm sorry, miss, but there is no one here under those names." Time freezes around me. I definitely have the right hospital. How could they not be here?

"Are you sure? I got a call telling me they were in an accident and were brought here."

"I will check again, just give me a moment." She types something else and frowns again. She gets up from the counter and goes to talk to a man with dark under eyes and rough stubble. They talk in hushed tones and throw me occasional concerned glances.

I look around the waiting room and try my best to keep my cool. How is it possible to have lost my fucking parents?

They both come back to where I am waiting, they give each other an awkward look before looking back at me. "Miss Locket, we are sorry, but we definitely do not have anyone in the hospital with those names."

I thank them, not knowing what the hell else I'm supposed to say and go back outside. I need to figure out what the fuck is going on here. I look up and down the insanely busy street. I take a seat on one of the benches and put my hands in my pockets. *What the fuck is going on?*

My phone begins ringing for the twentieth time today. And just as I have every other time when I see Alexander's name on the caller ID, I hang up. I glance quickly at his latest message, begging me to let him know I'm okay and demanding to know where I am.

I dismiss Alexander's messages and decide on a plan to settle this once and for all. I go back to my car and make the half-hour drive to my parents' house.

***

"Sammie, what are you doing here?" My mother is standing in the doorframe, watching me get out of my car. Her deepening smile lines deepen around her eyes, and her signature bold red lips sit upon a perfect teeth smile.

"You're okay? What about Dad? Is he alright?"

"We are both fine, sweetheart. Come inside, you look all out of sorts. Tell me what's going on."

We walk into my childhood home. It smells of bleach, mums been deep cleaning again. She flicks the kettle on and starts setting up to make coffee. I take a seat at the kitchen island and watch as she loads the sugar and coffee into the mugs.

"Sammie, what's happened. Yesterday you were on the Gold Coast, and if I'm remembering right, you were supposed to be gone for two weeks?" She places one of the coffees in front of me and excuses herself while she takes the other outside to do who, as always, is in the shed he converted into a man cave. I can't tell her anything about what's wrong, not even why I'm back. How to I explain that for some reason I got a call from someone saying they had both been in an accident? What was even gained from such a sick joke? I'm down seven hundred dollars because of the last-minute ticket, and I haven't even been able to tell Alisha I'm not in the same damn city as her anymore.

She comes back in, and she narrows her eyes at my nervous, nail-biting habit.

"So?" she says, raising her eyebrow.

"I have an interview for a job I applied for; I can't risk passing it up." There, I think it went well enough. My cheeks didn't go red, I didn't stutter over my words, and I kept pretty decent eye contact.

"Where is the job?"

Fuck.

"A cleaning job for a lady who cleans homes for a living. It's different from anything I've done before, but at this point, I will take whatever I can get."

She purses her lips but doesn't press any further. I know better than to think this is the end of this conversation; it's just on pause.

"I'm making lasagna for dinner. You're helping." I would argue, but I know better than that. Plus, it's such a rare event that I have the time to join Mum in the kitchen these days. It's something we did together at least once a week since I was eight, right up until I moved out at eighteen. Of everything she got right with me as a parent, teaching me to cook is the one thing I plan on passing on to my eventual children in the exact same way she did.

"I would love to, Mum."

Twenty

Dinner with my parents was a very welcome distraction, although temporary. They're planning on taking off over Christmas to South Australia. They intend on taking the long way back, meaning they will circle around through the Northern Territory, Queensland, and New South Wales. Part of me was sad that it means they won't be home for Christmas, and try as I might, I did try to play it off like I didn't mind, but Mum, as she always does, knew better. I know she's going to call me leading up to it, asking if I want them to delay leaving, but only after dad has already called to tell me they are going when they had already planned, and that's final, so do my best to convince her I don't need them here.

I navigate through my dimly lit house, illuminated only by golden hour. The sun's brilliant orange casts beautiful cascades of light against the walls. It almost looks as if the walls are on fire.

The night air coming through the windows in my farmhouse is freezing. I slump down onto my sofa and pinch the bridge of my nose in a useless attempt to ease the building tension. The quiet seclusion of my home, where I usually find solace unlike anywhere else, leaves me feeling incredibly broken and offers none of its usual comfort.

I have never in my life questioned what I would do in a situation where I faced a dead or dying person. Finding out that I'm the type of person to walk away is reshaping everything I thought I knew about myself. I want to lose my shit at Alexander for letting me think he was someone he isn't. I want to scream at Alisha for sending me on this fucking holiday in the first place. I put my head in my hands, and warm tears start to free flow. I'm pissed at them, all but more than that, I hate myself. I have how stupid and naive I was and how much of a coward I am.

My phone rings once again. I don't need to look. I know who it is. I can't speak to him. There is nothing for him to explain away. There was a man in his office shot in the head. There isn't a thing he can say to fix any of this. As much as a bigger than I am willing to admit part of me wants to give him the chance to explain I can't bring myself to answer him.

I flop back on the sofa with my head on the arm and fold my arms over my eyes. *I need to call the police.* I know I do but just as I can't bring myself to answer when he calls, I can't be the one to do something about it.

A splitting headache hits out of nowhere on the top of my head. the smell of iron becomes apparent,

Page | 288

but before I can figure out why, everything goes black.

***

"I just don't understand why we have to do this. She's supposed to be your best friend." The familiar voice says from somewhere to my right.

Something is wrong. I'm not on the sofa anymore. I fight the urge to open my eyes, not wanting them to know I'm awake. I do my best to discreetly figure out what exactly is going on. My head is pounding; the room smells of smoke, and I can hear the crackling of the fire to my right as well as feel its warmth. I'm in a seat with something tying me to it. I am assuming it's rope and I am tied around my arms, so they are pinned at my side as well as pinned back against the seat.

"You are such a fucking coward. Just go wait in the kitchen. I will deal with her. I don't want you doing something stupid like trying to intervene." My eyes fly open at the sound of her voice. She is dressed in black jeans, a black hoodie and boots. Her blonde hair is tied back into a ponytail, and she looks like she hasn't slept in days.

"Alisha, what the fuck?" I spit at her.

She saunters over to me with a Cheshire grin. "Sleeping Beauty is finally awake! I've missed you!"

I pull against my restraints.

"Oh, no, no, no." She clicks her tongue and shakes her head. "There will be none of that. I just need to ask you some questions. You make it easy on me; I make it easy on you."

My eyes widen in disbelief. I don't recognise a thing about the woman in front of me. There is no sign of my best friend who has sat across from me eating dinner, no sign of the girl who I've laughed with, drank with, or even argued with.

"Logan!" I cry out. My cheek stings from the feeling of her hand connecting with it.

She just fucking slapped me.

"He's not going to help you, Sammie, no one is coming to help you. You're a whore, not some damsel in need of rescuing. A whore who needs to be taught some fucking manners."

Oh my god, she's Logan's ex-girlfriend. She has to be. Why else would she know Logan? Why else would she be calling me a whore when he is the first man I've been with in over a year?

"This is because of Alexander?" It still doesn't feel right to use his name. images of the dead body flash behind my eyelids. I shake my head in an attempt to shake away the memory.

"I'm the one asking the questions. You have had your fun, taking *my* life and playing pretend while being on *my* holiday." She picks up one of my kitchen knives that, for reasons I don't even want to think about, is on my coffee table. She pokes at the pointed end with her index finger. "God, you just ruined *everything*!" She steps towards me, and I instinctively curl in on myself as much as the rope will allow. "I had everything planned out so perfectly. The seats on the plane, the hotel room. He just needed to see me again, I just needed the opportunity to talk to him, and he would have come to his senses and taken me back."

Holy shit, I'm right, she is his stalker ex-girlfriend. How could I have not known they were together?

Holy fuck, I did know. This is him! This is the guy she was seeing, who she was going to move to be with, that she wouldn't tell us anything about. This is on her! How was I supposed to know her master fucking plan when she never even showed me a picture of the fucking guy?

"Alisha, this is insane. How the fuck was I supposed to know who it was or that you were never planning on actually running away together to have a life break? The whole thing was a way for you to act like a fucking psycho and stalk him instead of picking up the phone like a normal person."

She throws the knife back down on the table and lets out a guttural, hate-filled scream.

"He wouldn't answer my calls, smart arse. Don't you think that's the first thing I would have done?"

She walks towards the fire and picks up the fire prod. I usually have it sitting up against the wall of the fireplace, but when she pulls it out, the end of it has been resting in the flames, and now the end of it is glowing red hot.

"Alisha, what the fuck? Put it down!" I plead. I search her face, looking desperately for my best friend hidden behind her blackened eyes and hate-filled grimace. There is nothing.

"Did you fuck him?"

My mouth falls open. What kind of sick question is that?

"Alisha, I'm not going to answer that. It's none of your fucking business."

She shrugs her shoulders. "Suit yourself." She places the still glowing rod against the skin on my arm. The smell of burned hair and the sound of my skin burning layer by layer makes me want to gag. I scream; tears immediately roll down my cheeks as the rod burns away layers of skin.

"Fine. Fine. Yes, we slept together." I scream at her, and she removes the rod, but it changes nothing. The searing pain continues.

"Now, that wasn't so hard, was it? Tell me what I want to know, and I won't need to make you." She says it so matter-of-factly, like we are having a conversation over coffee. It makes my stomach twist.

"Right, next —" she is cut off by her phone ringing in her pocket. She pulls it out, and the Cheshire grin is back. She holds her finger up at me to tell me to wait, and she hits the loudspeaker button.

"Autumn, what have you done. Where is she?"

It's Alexander! After everything that has happened today, I never imagined I would be relieved to hear his voice.

But he called her Autumn. The realisation smacks me in the face. Oh my god, she used a fake fucking name while she was with him!

"You don't need to worry about her anymore. I'm — taking care of it." She absent-mindedly picks the knife back up."

"Autumn, this has gone too far. You don't need to hurt her."

"Of course I do. It'd be the only way to make sure she's not going to get between us again."

There is a long, quiet pause.

She is impatiently pacing around the room, and I take the window of opportunity I have to try to wiggle one of my arms free.

"Tell me where you are." He sounds tired and defeated.

"I'm not that stupid, Alexander. Don't insult me."

By some miracle, the rope loosens around my right arm. She turns back towards me, and I stop moving and do my best to not let the rope sag where I've loosened it.

"Autumn, you will do as you are told." That voice, it's the same gravelly voice he was using when we were together last night. I fight the urge to throw up. Holy fuck, this is twisted.

"Alisha, he killed someone! He shot someone in his office this morning. He is dangerous." I don't even know why I told her. Maybe because I needed to stop hearing Alexander talk to her in that way, or because I saw the way a satisfied look washed over her face as he spoke.

She laughs at me, a sickening laugh that I've never heard from her before. Then she pulls a hand-gun from behind her back she had hidden in the top of her jeans.

"That wasn't Alexander Sammie, it was me." Disbelief washes over me. *It wasn't Alexander.*

She puts the phone down on the table and re-places it with the knife. "Now, shut the fuck up, I'm trying to have a conversation, and you're being rude."

Pain like nothing I have ever felt before courses through me, starting at my thigh. I cry out and stare in utter shock at the knife sticking out of the top of my thigh. Darkness plays at the corners of my vi-sion, and the room begins to spin. *I'm going to black out.*

"Tell me where you are so I can come get you, Autumn. You're right. I was a fucking idiot for letting you go. I can bring you home with me, and we can go back to being exactly as we were." Alexander's words make my stomach turn.

My front door slams open, and Logan rounds the corner into my living room.

"Logan please." I plead with him.

"Logan, I swear to God if you touch her, your daughter will not see her seventh birthday. Back. The fuck. Off."

He hesitates in the doorways. His eyes flicking from me to her.

"I'm at her house. I know you have her address, and I know you're in the area. I'm so glad you're coming to your senses, baby!"

I watch as Logan takes a step towards me. Indecision washes over his face, but in a split second, it's gone, and he is crossing the room towards me. relief fills every part of me. relief that Alexander didn't kill someone, relief that she is getting what she wants, so this can all end and relief that Logan is about to finally free me of this fucking chair.

A deafening bang makes my ears ring and my vision blur, but I can see enough to make out Logan on the floor, clutching his stomach as flood quickly begins to soak through his white shirt.

"No!" I cry out. Heavy heaving sobs and guilt escape me.

"I will see you soon!" Alisha says happily into the phone like she didn't just fucking shoot a man. She steps over his writhing body and directly in front of me.

She bends down so our eyes are level and tucks my hair behind my ear.

"No hard feelings, Sammie. I had to do what was necessary to make him come to his senses." She grabs the tip of the knife and slowly twists. I don't want to give her the satisfaction of crying or screaming, so I bite down on my lip. "All of this could have been avoided if you had of kept your hands to yourself. You brought all of this on yourself. And now, Logan and Marcus. Their deaths are on your head," she lets go of the knife and flashes a toothy smile.

"Oh, I'm going to need those boots for a little while longer. Let's be honest. They look better on me anyway, and Alexander is going to *love* them up on his shoulders when we —"

I plunge the knife into her stomach. Her eyes widen, and she starts making a strange gurgling sound when she tries to breathe. I watch as she falls to the floor in front of me. Emotion, pain, guilt, despair, it all washes over me like a tidal wave that's trying to pull me under and flood out my lungs. I scream and cry out until the room goes almost completely black. I look down at the blood spewing from my thigh. *That's not good.*

My head falls back just as I hear someone run into the house.

"Fuck!" I can vaguely make out the feeling of the ropes loosening as I get freed. Warm arms pick me up from the chair, and I rest my head against his chest and breathe him in.

It's him.

"Alexander." I'm not sure if I actually managed to say his name or just imagined it.

"I'm here, baby, I've got you. The ambulance is on its way."

I do my best to keep my eyes open and stay awake, but the best I can do is occasional flashes of being aware of my surroundings. Alexander has put me on the sofa, and something has been tied way too tightly around my thigh. I don't know how much time passes, but the sound of the ambulance and police fills the room, and the next time I come to, I am riding in the back of the ambulance. Alexander is looking down at me, he is frowning, his eyes are red, and his cheeks are tear-stained. I can just make out the feeling of him squeezing my hand and the sound of him begging me to stay awake.

Twenty-One

Alexander traces the burn scar on my arm. The constant memory of Alisha's actions, etched into my body, confirms that it was real, not a nightmare. Every time I try to wrap my head around everything that happened that night, I send myself into an anxiety attack. I thought I knew her. We had been best friends for years. We spent so much time together. Dinner, movies, sleepovers, and road trips. I never once thought it would be possible for her to become so completely unrecognisable. More than that, I never thought it would be possible for her to hurt me.

"We have to get out of bed." He murmurs and traces light kisses along my jaw and brings me back out of my spiralling thoughts.

"You could stay here for another day?" I already know he can't. He has pushed back so many meetings as it is, and the board is getting *difficult.*

"Come with me. Please. I want nothing more than to come home to you every evening. I hate that I have to keep leaving you here alone." He has gotten so used to me saying no and shutting him down. And until now, I have meant it. We are still finding our feet as a couple, and after everything that happened, I needed to make sure that being with him is something I really want. Plus, it has taken me until now to even be able to face Logan. No amount of his insisting he doesn't regret what he did will ever make me comfortable with him choosing to risk his and his daughter's life to save mine. His daughter, of course, was always fine. Alisha had just made him think she had hidden herself away when actually she was with her mother, visiting family.

"Fine, let's get out of bed. I will put the kettle on." I plant a kiss on the top of his head that makes his cheeks warm.

I'm careful not to put too much weight on my leg. It's on its way to being healed, but there is still a long road to go until I'm completely on the mend.

I tie my robe around me and go to head downstairs.

"Nothing but underwear under your robe, Miss Locket. You're spoiling me to one of my favourite outfits of yours."

I roll my eyes at him and go downstairs to make the coffee.

I find the letter I need from the mail basket, finish making the coffees and put the letter beside his coffee.

Alexander comes downstairs. He is wearing black jeans, a charcoal suit jacket, and a black tie. He has his go bag packed and ready in his hand.

Usually, the sight of it would ruin my entire mood. He sits at the kitchen island. I pick up my coffee and take a sip, trying my best to hide my smile.

"What's this?" He asks as he opens it.

I watch as his eyes widen and a huge face splitting smile plants on his face.

"You got a job in Brisbane? When did you even apply for this? Wait. So, you're saying yes to moving in with me?"

I shake my head at his barrage of questions. "Yes, I got a job. I start in two weeks. Yes, Alexander, I'm saying I will move in with you." I take another sip of my coffee. "We will have to travel back for court dates, but it's a temporary problem." I do my best to ignore the tensing of his jaw. "And I applied while I was on holiday." My words come out rushed.

He is out of the stool and in front of me, his lips firmly against mine in an instant.

"You are impossible, Samantha Locket, and as always, I continue to find myself in awe of you."

"Right back at you, Mr Truette." I smile at him.

I'm suddenly not in the mood for coffee anymore. I step back from him and untie my robe. An appreciative moan escapes him. "My little Siren." He murmurs and lifts me onto the island.

About the Author

J. A. Garth is an author from Qld, Australia, who has a passion for fantasy novels that get you lost in another world, crime thrillers that keep you on the edge of your seat and dark romances that make you quiver. Born in 1996, with a love for reading for about that same amount of time. She has dreamt of joining her author heroes since she was a little girl. After moving to Qld from Victoria at 16, she worked various jobs, including cleaning and being a barista/waitress. By the time she was 23, she was married, had her first three children and published her first novel.

When she isn't working on a new project, she enjoys resting with a good book, watching sitcoms, true crime documentaries or alien conspiracies. And expanding her sometimes good, but most of the time not so good, cooking skills.